Through the Night
and
Such Impossibilities

Two Plays for Television

by

TREVOR GRIFFITHS

FABER AND FABER

3 Queen Square

London

First published in 1977
by Faber and Faber Limited
3 Queen Square London WC1
Printed in Great Britain by
Unwin Brothers Limited Old Woking Surrey
All rights reserved

© 1977 by Trevor Griffiths

All applications for performing rights should be
addressed to Clive Goodwin Associates, 79 Cromwell Road,
London, SW7 5BN

British Library Cataloguing in Publication Data

Griffiths, Trevor
    Through the night ; and, Such impossibilities.
    I. Title
    822'.9'14   PR6057.R52T/

    ISBN 0-571-11158-0

Of all the outlets available to a playwright for his work, television seems to me at once the most potent and the most difficult; the most potent and *therefore* the most difficult, one's inclined to add. Film boasts a 'global audience' (as one celebrated English director put it, perhaps as a way of justifying his new Californian existence) but has never afforded the writer a status in the power-structure much above that of, say, a second-unit director. With relatively few exceptions, film uses (and has usually always attracted) writers for whom wealth[*] and ease and a certain sort of localised (i.e. American) celebrity are or have become inseparable from the writing impulse itself; so that the consequential loss of regard (and self-regard) will be measured against more tangible and presumably more consumable gains. The global audience will then be surrendered by the writer to the expert ministrations of other 'ideas men': studio chiefs ('We could have bought into North Sea oil with what we paid for this shit'), distributors ('It's too long/short/frank'), directors ('Do I get the cut?'), stars ('I *know* what they want. They want me.') and so on.

Theatre is in important ways the converse; that's to say, while at its most secure it offers the writer a greater degree of control than any other medium over the production of his work, it is incapable, as a social

[*] The current top-price for a screenplay that's made into a film is around 400,000 dollars and perhaps 5% of the gross profit. Most screenplays are never made, of course; another aspect of writer's impotence.

institution, of reaching, let alone *mobilising*, large
popular audiences, at least in what is more and more
desperately referred to as the Free World. Success in the
theatre can confer fame, prestige, wealth, critical
acclaim and a place in literature, but all of them will
be pickled in a sort of class aspic. To write only for
the theatre is to watch only from the covered stand; you
stay dry but there's a pitch dividing you from another
possible, and possibly decisive, action on the terraces.

There are fewer cinemagoers in Britain now than there
are anglers; fewer regular theatregoers than car-rallyers.
For most people, plays are television plays, 'drama' is
television drama (though it's a word used almost
exclusively by those responsible for *production*, rarely
if ever by audiences). A play on television, transmitted
in mid-evening on a weekday, will make some sort of
contact with anything from three to twelve million people
(twenty if it's a series), usually all at the same time.
And the *potential* audience, because of television's
irreversibly network nature, is every sighted person in the
society with a set and the time and desire to watch. Not
surprisingly, a medium as potentially dangerous as this
one will need to be *controlled* with some rigour and
attention to detail. 'To inform' and 'to educate' may
well be in the charter alongside 'to entertain', but
information that inflames and education that subverts will
find its producers facing unrenewed contracts and its
contributors mysteriously dropped. (Who took the
decision, and on what grounds, not to repeat the brilliant
Days of Hope? Or not to renew the contract of Kenith Trodd,
producer of *Leeds United* and the suppressed *Brimstone &
Treacle*?) It would be odd, of course, if it were
otherwise. In a society predicated on the exploitation of

the many by the few, in a world a large part of which
operates according to precisely the same capitalist
principle, yet where the necessary tactical avowal of
democratic process has led to its actualisation, however
shallowly, and not always so, in the minds and actions of
the exploited, the shaping of consciousness, the erection
of the superstructure of consent, will become the major
cultural concern of the state and the dominant class or
classes it represents. What Enzensberger calls 'the
consciousness industry' (cf. H. M. Enzensberger: 'The
Industrialization of the Mind' in *Raids & Reconstructions*,
Pluto Press, 1976) has become, more than steel, coal or oil
or motorcars, the critical industry in the efficient
management of modern societies, capitalist and Stalinist
alike; as television has increasingly come to be located
as that industry's key sector.

The constraints and difficulties of writing for
television can then be easily described. Certain sorts of
'language', certain sorts of subject, certain sorts of
form - an urban terrorist saying 'Fuck off' straight to
camera pithily embodies all three - will inevitably
trigger discreetly placed control - mechanisms on the
floor above the floor you're working on. And a writer's
arguments *ad rem* or *hominem* will never be enough to
overcome the blandly prepared positions of a Television
Controller. (Theatres have directors; films have chiefs;
only television has the need and the confidence to let
nomenclature reveal function in this way.) Yet in
important ways, the experience cannot be reduced to the
simple equation of company diktat = writer's accommodation,
as many talented writers and intellectuals of the left
have for too long tried to assert, in a puny apology for a
theory of the media. For one thing, as Enzensberger

points out, a communications system beyond a critical size cannot continue to be centrally controlled and must then be dealt with statistically. 'This basic "leakiness" of stochastic* systems admittedly allows the calculation of probabilities based on sampling and extrapolations; but blanket supervision would demand a monitor that was bigger than the system itself.... A censor's office, which carried out its work extensively, would of necessity become the largest branch of industry in its society.' Moreover, direct leakage is not the only sort: for example, the 'meanings' or 'messages' of plays are often encoded in such a way that the controllers of television output are incapable of decoding them with any precision. (In particular I'm thinking of plays where working-class idioms, speech patterns, behaviours suggest one thing but imply, by defensively developed irony, something quite other, which only a person of that class or with a deep knowledge of it could be expected to recognise readily. I suspect much of *Bill Brand* worked in very much that way, with a working-class audience.)

To argue, then, as many still do, that television is part of a *monolithic* consciousness industry where work of truly radical or revolutionary value will never be produced is at once to surrender to undialectical thought and to fail to see the empirical evidence there is to refute such an argument. If the medium weren't of the highest critical importance in the building and maintenance of the structures of popular consent, there'd be no need for controllers; conversely, the presence and activity of controllers rigorously monitoring and modifying the nature of the output is one index among many

*   i.e. systems based on *conjecture* rather than certainty.

of the medium's importance. To work in television as a
playwright will be to seek to exploit the system's basic
'leakiness', so as to speak intimately and openly, with
whatever seriousness and relevance one can generate, to
(though it must in time be *with*) the many millions of
cohabitants of one's society who share part of a language,
part of a culture, part of a history, with oneself; as not
so to work, the opportunity *there*, will be to settle for
less, a sheltering myopia or praise from the cell.

And let there be no cant, finally, about television's
'moving wallpaper', about 'advertising fodder' and the
'manipulable masses' and all the rest of the sad copy of
minds tired of the problem and eager for revenge on those
who would not listen. 'The "telly-glued" masses do not
exist; they are the bad fiction of our second-rate social
analysts. What the masses, old or new, might do is
anybody's guess. But the actual men and women, under
permanent kinds of difficulty, will observe and learn, and
I do not think that in the long run they will be anybody's
windfall.' The words are Raymond Williams's and, as with
so much he has written in the last twenty-five years, I
wish they were mine.

The two plays contained in this volume were conceived
and written for television. *Through the Night* was
transmitted on BBC-1 on 2 December 1975, to an estimated
audience of more than eleven million people, and is
scheduled to be repeated in August of this year. Close to
a hundred phone calls were 'logged' by the BBC's duty
officer on the night of its broadcast; the producer's
office and *Radio Times* received a heavy postbag during the
following weeks; and I received personal mail amounting to
some 180 letters. The *Sunday People* opened its columns to
readers inviting them to send in their own experiences of

mastectomy treatment. More than 1,800 letters were received over the next ten days. Few critics saw (or at least wrote about) the piece; and the critic of *The Observer* spoke for many, perhaps, when he said: 'I found this week's episode of *The Nearly Man* by Arthur Hopcraft sufficient excuse for not watching *Through the Night* (BBC-1), a Trevor Griffiths play about breast cancer which I lacked the nerve to face.' It is, without question, my best-known piece.

Such Impossibilities was written in 1971, commissioned by the BBC as part of a series entitled *The Edwardians*. Though I had explained at some length what I wanted to write, the play was rejected and has never been seen. The ostensible grounds were cost – they often are – but it's at least as likely that the play offered too brutal and too overtly political a contrast with the remainder of the series, which included, if you remember, pieces on E. Nesbit, the Countess of Warwick, Marie Lloyd, Baden-Powell, Conan Doyle, Horatio Bottomley, Rolls-Royce and Lloyd George. Tom Mann might well have roughed the series up a bit, but it's arguable he might also have done something towards redressing its 'balance' too. Still, it must count, till now at least, as a failure. Should it ever be produced, it can then be tested against the severest of its intentions: to restore, however tinily, an important but suppressed area of our collective history; to enlarge our 'usable past' and connect it with a lived present; and to celebrate a victory.

Trevor Griffiths
Leeds, 14 February 1977

THROUGH THE NIGHT

Through the Night was first shown on BBC TV in December 1975. The cast was as follows:

CHRISTINE POTTS	Alison Steadman
DR PEARCE	Jack Shepherd
MR STAUNTON	Tony Steedman
DR SEAL	Thelma Whiteley
MRS SCULLY	Anne Dyson
ANNA JAY	Julia Schofield
JOE POTTS	Dave Hill
SISTER WARREN	Andonia Katsaros
NURSE O'MALLEY	Phylomena McDonagh
STAFF NURSE BRENTON	Sheila Kelly
NURSE CHATTERJEE	Rebecca Mascarenhas
REGISTRAR	Richard Wilson
NIGHT SISTER	Patricia Leach
THEATRE SISTER	Wendy Wax
NIGHT NURSES	Sue Elgin, Angela Bruce, Anna Mottram
ANAESTHETIST	John Rowe
DR MOUNT	Richard Ireson
LUCY	Jeillo Edwards
PORTER	Louis Cabot
MRS GOODWIN	Anna Wing
MARTHA PAISLEY	Jane Freeman
OUTPATIENTS SISTER	Rachel Davies
AUXILIARY	Barbara Ashcroft
TEA-LADY	Shirley Allen
RELIGIOUS VISITOR	Peter Lawrence

MOTHER	Kathleen Worth
WOMAN PATIENT	Myrtle Devenish
JOAN	Jeanne Doree
AGNES	Lucy Griffiths

Script Editor	Colin Tucker
Designer	Sue Spence
Producer	Ann Scott
Director	Michael Lindsay-Hogg

1.   INT.   EXAMINATION ROOM.   DAY

LS CHRISTINE POTTS, around thirty, in examination room of
large general hospital. She wears a white cotton gown
over skirt, etc: is naked from waist up beneath it.
CHRISTINE sits on a canvas chair, alone, in the bottle-
bright room. She listens.

From the next room, through the thin wood wall, the oddly
distinct sounds of an examination being conducted.
The connecting door opens suddenly and a SISTER, spruce,
young, bright, appears. She carries a small bunch of
brown open files in her arms.

SISTER: *(Studying top file cover)* Are you ready, Mrs ...
   Potts? The doctor will be with you presently.
   (The SISTER smiles, withdraws immediately.
   CHRISTINE feels her breast, catches sight of herself in
   a glass cupboard filled with instruments.
   The connecting door opens and the SISTER returns,
   leading in the examination team.)
   This is Mrs Potts, Mr Staunton.
   (She hands STAUNTON the file. To CHRISTINE:) Would
   you just lie on here for me, Mrs Potts. And we'll
   have this off for a moment, shall we? *(The SISTER*
   removes the gown, helps CHRISTINE on to the black
   leather couch.) There we are ...
   (STAUNTON, the consultant, has been studying the file.
   He's tall, gaunt, around sixty; wears a three-piece
   pin-stripe suit, discreet tie, half-glasses over which
   he appears to do most of his seeing.
   As he steps to the examination couch he hands the file

to the blonde house surgeon on his right, who (when she's read it) hands it to the other member of the team, a young houseman with three days growth of stubble on his face and longish hair, tatty white coat and basketball shoes. The young houseman wears a T-shirt (i.e. no tie) under his coat.)

STAUNTON: Well, Mrs Potts. Let's see what we have here, shall we. *(He feels the left breast with both hands, palpating the lump. Measuring it, tracing gland paths up into the armpit.)* Yes. Yes. Yes. Yes. Now. You discovered it when?

CHRISTINE: Erm. About three weeks ago, doctor. Just after Christmas I think it were ...

STAUNTON: Yes. And when did you get round to seeing your doctor?

CHRISTINE: Well, I went that week.

STAUNTON: *(Pausing fractionally)* I see. Yes.

CHRISTINE: *(Helpfully)* I've been waiting to be seen ...

STAUNTON: Yes. *(To house surgeon, low, confidential, patient-excluding voice:)* Tell me what you think, Doctor Seal.

(DOCTOR SEAL moves into his space, feeling breast thoroughly, examining it visually. She speaks over her shoulder to the consultant.)

DOCTOR SEAL: No pain, so we can probably rule out a cyst. Clearly not a haematoma. Absence of discharge suggests it's not an intraduct papilloma ... I think we can rule out fat necrosis ... More likely fibroadenoma ... At this age particularly, sir ...

(DOCTOR SEAL smiles, steps back.

STAUNTON looks at the houseman.)

STAUNTON: Is that a *beard* you're growing, Doctor Pearce?

PEARCE: I suppose it is really, Mr Staunton.

18

STAUNTON: Would you care to give an opinion?
    (PEARCE comes forward slowly, some unexplained
    resistance in him to the procedure.)
PEARCE: *(Smiling)* Hello, Mrs Potts.
    (CHRISTINE smiles, a little uncertainly.)
    Would you mind if I examined your breast?
    (PEARCE speaks in an unsmoothed Leeds voice:
    undoctorlike.)
CHRISTINE: No doctor ...
    (PEARCE begins his examination. Finishes it.)
PEARCE: Thank you. *(He hands CHRISTINE the gown, to cover*
    her chest with.) Has it grown at all, since you first
    noticed it, Mrs Potts?
CHRISTINE: Yes, it has, doctor. It were quite a bit
    smaller ...
    (Pause)
STAUNTON: Ideas?
PEARCE: *(Looking at CHRISTINE)* It's all a bit
    speculative, isn't it? I don't think I'd want to rule
    out neoplasm.
    (STAUNTON looks quickly at CHRISTINE, to reassure
    himself the word has no meaning for her. Frowns at
    PEARCE.
    The SISTER opens the connecting door, speaks to the
    woman in the next room.)
SISTER: Are you ready, Mrs ... Banton? The doctor will
    be with you presently. *(Returns, closing door silently.)*
STAUNTON: Yes. *(Pause. Practised smile at patient.)*
    Right you are, Mrs Potts. We'll arrange for you to
    come in so that we can do a tiny operation and find
    out what it is.
CHRISTINE: Will it be for long, doctor? I've two little
    girls, you see ...

STAUNTON: A couple of days. I don't think there's
      anything to worry about ... *(To SISTER.)* Biopsy, sister.
      (The SISTER asks with her pen which of two columns
      this should be entered under.)
      Non-urgent.
      (The SISTER copies it into file.)
      I'll see you again, Mrs Potts ...
      (They file out behind the SISTER.
      PEARCE winks at CHRISTINE as he leaves.)
PEARCE: All right?
      (CHRISTINE smiles, grateful.)
CHRISTINE: Doctor Paignton said he were sure it were
      nothing ...
PEARCE: I'm sure Doctor Paignton knows what he's talking
      about.
      (PEARCE leaves, closing the door behind him.
      CHRISTINE sits up, stands. LS. She looks down at her
      breast.
      Quite audible, the next examination starting up in the
      next room.)

2. INT. WARD. DAY
Ward 20 (Women's Surgical). Mid-morning. Several discrete
but overlapping actions convey the mood and sense of the
place:
Mid-morning tea is being served by a young West Indian
woman with ornamental spectacles: a SENIOR REGISTRAR
(George) and DOCTOR SEAL are studying a patient's
(MRS GOODWIN's) notes at the bottom of the ward.
PEARCE and a NURSE are taking a history from a newly
admitted woman with acute appendicitis; a woman in a
wheelchair, happy, well looking, is slowly pushed along
the ward by an ambulance man on her way home; pupil nurse

CHATTERJEE, slim, small, girlish, Indian, does temperatures
as though the system's reputation depended on it.
CHRISTINE arrives at the top of the ward, in nightdress
and nylon quilted dressing gown.

TEA LADY: *(Local accent)* No sugar, Joan. How you like it.

JOAN: *(Old, gaunt)* Bless you, Maria, bless you. I'm fair
    clemming.

    (TEA LADY, delicately placing it, quiet, matter-of-fact.)

TEA LADY: How was the stout?

JOAN: Grand. Gave me the runs.

TEA LADY: Said it would.

    (The REGISTRAR and SEAL with MRS GOODWIN, opposite
    sides of the bed. They talk across the old lady, who
    follows them with her eyes as they knock up.)

REGISTRAR: *(Studying file)* Looks like another one ...

SEAL: Yes, I think so.

REGISTRAR: Who did the last one? *(Thumbing a file.)* Oh I
    did. *(He smiles at SEAL.)* All these years. Let it be
    a lesson, doctor. Can't win 'em all.

SEAL: Seven years. I don't call that bad.

    (A burst of laughter from across the ward. They turn
    to look.)

    Mrs Paisley. Going home.

REGISTRAR: His nibs'll be pleased.

SEAL: He *is*.

    (MRS PAISLEY talking to a cluster of ambulants in the
    sink and table area.)

MRS PAISLEY: *(About fifty, ruddy complexion)* ... You're
    not kidding. If the old feller ever finds out where
    they've had their hands, he'll never speak to me
    again. *(Laughing unforcedly.)* Still, what he doesn't
    know won't hurt him. I'll see you at the Three Tuns
    a week Satday, Agnes ...

AGNES: *(Pale, thin)* Nay, I'm not so sure, Martha ...

MRS PAISLEY: Don't be daft, course I will, I'll get you a port in - and I don't drink port - so you'd better be there. Bye, bye, bye, bye, Carmel, Mildred, Kath ... *(A chorus of 'Bye Martha ...' as MRS PAISLEY trundles up the ward.)*

JOAN: *(Calling, remembering)* Don't forget your boyfriend now, Martha ...

(MRS PAISLEY turns, grins.)

MRS PAISLEY: Don't be naughty!

(MRS PAISLEY arrives at the bed area where PEARCE and a NURSE take the history.)

PEARCE: *(To patient)* What would you say, all the time, every so often, once in a while, what?

WOMAN: Phww. I don't rightly know. Sometimes it's all the time, sometimes it's now and again. Then again every so often it's just once in a while ...

(PEARCE frowns, clears his throat, looks across at the NURSE.)

PEARCE: *(Slowly)* Did you get all that, nurse?

MRS PAISLEY: *(OOV)* I'm just off now, Doctor. Come to say goodbye.

PEARCE: Excuse me. *(He walks towards MRS PAISLEY.)* Oh, you're off then, sexpot? What am I supposed to do at nights now, eh? *(To ambulance man.)* Watch this one, Peter. She'll have your pants off as you push her ...

MRS PAISLEY: Here, that'll do. I've a husband and four kids ...

PEARCE: It's not all you've got, Martha. *(He kisses MRS PAISLEY's cheek. Very serious:)* Take ... care. *(He's close to her face. She looks at him in silence.)* Terra.

MRS PAISLEY: Terra.

(PEARCE watches MRS PAISLEY up the ward before turning
back to his patient.
We see CHRISTINE still in doorway, stepping aside to
let MRS PAISLEY pass.)
Cheer up, lass. Naught to be feared of.
(A clean, plain, pleasant smile.
CHRISTINE smiles back, rather timid.
The doors slap behind her, she pushes into the ward,
past CHATTERJEE, the tea trolley, PEARCE, until she
reaches her bed, the number of which she checks before
surveying it and the area and furniture about it.
NURSE O'MALLEY arrives, carrying a cheap plastic
suitcase.)

O'MALLEY: Here it is, Mrs Potts. Your clothes is here,
    ready for your man this evening. He can bring 'em in
    when you're ready for home.

SISTER: *(OOV)* Nurse O'Malley!

O'MALLEY: Coming, sister! *(To CHRISTINE.)* Better slip into
    bed for a while, Mrs Potts. Best place, out of the way.
    (NURSE O'MALLEY slips the case behind the locker,
    joins SENIOR SISTER WARREN and STAFF NURSE BRENTON,
    who are directing the theatre porter where to place a
    trolley. On it, on blood drip, MRS SCULLY, late
    sixties, very thin, white, still under anaesthetic.
    Who could be dead.
    The PORTER is very young, in tight-fitting jeans, a
    'Save the Watergate 5000' T-shirt and plimsolls.
    Grubby white coat, open and torn. Straight light
    brown hair a good six inches beyond his shoulders.
    SISTER WARREN, blonde hair, black roots, amazingly
    spruce in white with black belt, court shoes and
    American style hat, supervises proceedings.
    MRS SCULLY is being returned to her bed next to

CHRISTINE's.

*Through all of this, LUCY, fat morose West Indian
cleaner, wetmops the ward floor.)*

WARREN: Watch those bottles.

*(The PORTER stares at WARREN as though she's just
revealed a long-suspected insanity.)*

PORTER: *(Guiding trolley in)* Them bottles'll see you out,
sister.

WARREN: I'd sooner they saw Mrs Scully out actually.

BRENTON: *(Short, chunky)* Right. Thank you. Screens,
nurse.

*(O'MALLEY draws the curtains on the rails that
surround the bed area.*

CHRISTINE's view has been replaced by green curtain.)

WOMAN'S VOICE: *(OOV)* Is this seven?

*(CHRISTINE turns. A young girl (ANNA JAY), nineteen
or twenty, in dressing gown and slippers, stands at
the bottom of next bed.)*

CHRISTINE: Yes, it will be. *(She turns to look at the
plastic number plate on the bed head.)* I'm eight.

ANNA: Oh yes. Thanks. *(She flops on to the bed.*

Surveying room:) God, what a dump.

*(CHRISTINE follows ANNA's eyes round the twenty or so
beds they can see. Their eyes meet eventually.)*

I'm in for a biopsy. I've got a lump on my breast.

CHRISTINE: Me too. I've just arrived.

ANNA: Snap. Anna Jay.

CHRISTINE: Christine Potts.

ANNA: I'm at the university.

CHRISTINE: Oh. *(Pause)* I'm a housewife.

ANNA: *(Surveying ward)* You wouldn't want to lance a *boil*
in a place like this, would you?

CHRISTINE: *(Not understanding)* It's my first time in

a hospital. I suppose they're pretty much alike.
(O'MALLEY jerks the curtains on MRS SCULLY's bed back
with a sharp scraping sound.
The PORTER begins skating his trolley back up the ward,
one foot propelling, the other resting on the rear
transverse strut.
The nurses disperse.)

WARREN: *(Passing ANNA's bed, not stopping)* I think you'd
be better in your bed, Miss Jay. *(To BRENTON.)* X-rays
for those two, Staff Nurse.
(BRENTON follows WARREN to the windowed nurses' room
at the top of the ward.
O'MALLEY stays at MRS SCULLY's bedside for a moment
scraping wisps of scraggy grey hair back from the
forehead.
ANNA stands, stares at MRS SCULLY's ashen face, the
drips.)

ANNA: Oh God.

3. INT. WARD. DAY

O'MALLEY dry-shaves CHRISTINE's armpit.
CHATTERJEE shaves ANNA's.
The food ritual has begun at the top of the ward, BRENTON
serving, nurses handing out.

O'MALLEY: *(To CHATTERJEE)* Ryan's up the spout.
(CHATTERJEE blank.)
Pregnant. Do you know Ryan? Third year, she's on 15.
(Pause) Sorry, did I hurt you? *(Pause)* Leaving at the
end of the month to get married. Lucky pig. *(Pause)*
Just got a job on agency too. Sixty quid a week
doing the same job she's doing now for peanuts.
(Pause) We muster been born mugs, Chatty.

CHATTERJEE: *(Serious innocent)* Don't you like it here?

4. INT. WARD. DAY

CHRISTINE dozes, mid-afternoon.

OOV, DR SEAL's voice, repeating 'Mrs Potts' several times.
She opens her eyes. The curtains have been drawn round
her bed.

SEAL sits on a chair by the bedside, the file on her knee.

SEAL: Having a nap, were we, Mrs Potts?

CHRISTINE: I must have dropped off, doctor.

SEAL: I'd like to take another look before tomorrow,
    Mrs Potts.

    (CHRISTINE slips her nightdress over her head. SEAL
    begins the examination.)

    How long ago was it we saw you?

CHRISTINE: Just coming up to three weeks, doctor.

SEAL: Yes. *(Still feeling.)* Still no pain?

CHRISTINE: No.

SEAL: Good. Yes. Good. *(She feels again under the*
    armpit.) Is it about the same size, would you say?

CHRISTINE: No. I think it's a bit bigger.

SEAL: Yes. Good. You can put your thing on now.

    (CHRISTINE puts the nightdress on. SEAL opens her
    file, finds a form, takes out her pen.)

    I'd like you to sign the consent form, Mrs Potts.
    (She hands the form in the file to CHRISTINE, and the
    pen.) We're not permitted to do anything without the
    patient's consent.

    (CHRISTINE does her best to read it.)

    It's just to say that you give your consent to the
    biopsy ...

CHRISTINE: *(Finding the word)* Biopsy ...

SEAL: Yes. We'll cut a piece of the lump and er do some
    tests on it ... and the tests will tell us what to do
    next, if anything. Sign there, if you will.

26

*(CHRISTINE signs on the line indicated. SEAL takes
the file and pen, stands.)*

Good. We'll see you tomorrow in theatre, Mrs Potts.

CHRISTINE: Thank you, doctor.

*(SEAL pulls the curtains back, revealing the ward,
inert and littered. Leaves.)*

ANNA: *(Watching her go)* She's the one with cold hands,
isn't she? Still, you know what they say, cold
hands ... *(She smiles, leaves it unspoken.)*
*(An old woman hobbles past on a Zimmer-frame, says
something neither of them catches.
MRS SCULLY begins to moan and mutter in the next bed.
She lies half-propped, eyes open, staring at the far
ceiling.)*

SCULLY: Oh the bastards. The bloody bastards. Oh the
bastards. They are. Bloody bastards. Wait till I
see him. He's nothing else.

5. INT. WARD. NIGHT

*CU JOE POTTS. Early thirties, broad, powerful, squat
face, balding, weather-beaten with big roughened hands.
He's a brickie, straight from work.*

Beyond him, the sounds of a busy evening visiting time.

JOE: The kids are all right. They're at your mother's.

(CHRISTINE purposive, alert, a different person.)

CHRISTINE: Linda'll need her dinner money on Monday, tell
her, if I'm not home. 60p.

JOE: I thought you said you'd be out Friday.

CHRISTINE: Well, you know what these places are. Who
took their clothes?

JOE: Your Renee met 'em from school. I left a key under
the brick.

CHRISTINE: Have you spoken to anyone?

JOE: How do you mean?

CHRISTINE: *Here.*

JOE: Oh. No.

CHRISTINE: Have a word with the sister 'fore you go.

JOE: What for?

CHRISTINE: Well ... Ask her if I'm going to be out
    Friday.

JOE: I thought they'd told you.

CHRISTINE: She won't bite you.

JOE: What's the point. I mean if she's told you ...
    They know what they're doing.
    (Silence.
    JOE shifts uneasily on his chair. Looks at the clock
    at the bottom of the ward.
    CHRISTINE looks over his shoulder at ANNA, who nuzzles
    her boy-friend's ear. At MRS SCULLY who sleeps.)
    What's wrong with *her.*

CHRISTINE: I don't know.
    (Silence)

JOE: When do you have it then?

CHRISTINE: Tomorrow morning. Sister says I'm first on
    the list.

JOE: Oh. Good. *(Pause)* Have you got everything you want?

CHRISTINE: Yes. Don't forget the case.

JOE: It hardly seems worth it, does it? I thought of
    calling in at t'Working Men's ...

CHRISTINE: *(Firm)* Take it. They said you've to take it.
    (Pause again.)

JOE: *(Finally)* Do you want your crisps?
    (CHRISTINE shakes her head.)
    I gave your mother two pounds. Is that all right?
    (CHRISTINE nods.) She said she didn't want it, but ...

CHRISTINE: Make sure you get something to *eat,* won't you?

28

JOE: Stop fussing. Bloodyell.

O'MALLEY: *(Arriving)* Temperature, Mrs Potts.

> *(O'MALLEY slots the thermometer under CHRISTINE's*
> *tongue, takes her pulse, studying watch.)*

6. INT. CORRIDOR. NIGHT

Pupil nurse CHATTERJEE ushers the last of the visitors
from the ward.

In the open corridor by the nurses' room, JOE lingers,
watching sister WARREN entering something in her report
book.

A surge of leavers blocks his view for a moment. When it
clears, she's picked up the phone. He leaves, the case in
his hand.

7. INT. WARD. NIGHT

In the ward, two ambulant patients help to vase assorted
flowers left behind by the visitors.

BRENTON is already giving out drugs from the trolley,
mainly sleeping pills. She's one up from ANNA's bed,
pouring water for a feeble old woman, helping her to take
her two capsules. She watches ANNA, who has taken foil
from her handbag, swallows a yellow pill with some water.
BRENTON moves to the foot of ANNA's bed, consults her
chart briefly.

BRENTON: Do you have anything, Miss Jay. There's
    nothing written up for you.

ANNA: How're you fixed for a couple of grammes of
    cannabis resin? That usually does the trick.

BRENTON: Could I ask what that pill was you just took?
    You're not supposed to take pills in here, you know,
    not unless they're given you, you were told when you
    came in.

ANNA: Nobody told me a thing. Believe me.

BRENTON: Well, you took a pill ...

ANNA: It wasn't a pill. It was *the* Pill.

(BRENTON looks at the chart again.)

BRENTON: Just a minute.

(CHRISTINE eats her crisps, sitting up.)

MRS SCULLY: Give us one will you love?

(CHRISTINE turns startled.)

CHRISTINE: Are you ... supposed to?

MRS SCULLY: Sod it, give us one. I'm starving.

*(CHRISTINE holds the bag out. SCULLY's white arm
extends waveringly, the hand emerges with seven or
eight. She pushes them into her mouth as WARREN and
BRENTON return to ANNA's bed.)*

WARREN: Staff Nurse Brenton tells me you're on the Pill.

ANNA: That's right.

WARREN: Oh Christ. That's another 5-day bed wasted.
Didn't anybody tell you?

ANNA: Tell me what?

WARREN: *(To BRENTON)* I'd better ring Rogers. *(Consults
watch.)* He'll have gone. And don't leave the drugs
trolley unattended in the middle of the ward again,
Staff Nurse. How many more times ... *(Across the ward
to O'MALLEY, cutting daffodil stalks:)* Nurse, leave
those, get a pan for Mrs Scully, she's throwing up ...
*(WARREN's gone. O'MALLEY rushes on to the scene.
Green bile drips from MRS SCULLY's mouth on to the
pillow and beyond.)*

O'MALLEY: God, you devil, you've been eating, haven't
you? What have you been eating? You know what I
told you ...

BRENTON: Sleeping tablets for you, Mrs Potts. A good
night's sleep for tomorrow.

CHRISTINE: I'm ... fine, thank you.

BRENTON: *(Placing them on locker)* There we are. Take
    them with some water ... *(She smiles, leaves. Studies
    MRS SCULLY's chart. Preparing Stemetil injection:)*
    You don't deserve any, Mrs Scully.

MRS SCULLY: Sod off.

    *(O'MALLEY, trying to sponge SCULLY's sickstreaked hair,
    smiles with pleasure to herself.)*

8. INT. WARD. NIGHT

Night lighting.

*Clock says 10.15. Coughing, low muttering, moaning,
creaking.*

*A NURSING AUXILIARY, small, old, dumpy, talks to ANNA,
who lies listening.*

*CHRISTINE is looking at a picture of her two children, 6
and 3.*

*AUXILIARY watching out for the night sister in nurses'
room.*

AUXILIARY: ... I prefer men's wards. They're just like
    babies, once you get 'em in. And there's always a
    chance of a flash here and there. Dirty buggers. The
    older the dirtier. Eeh, they're always so grateful
    ... I like nights though. It's a rest from the old
    feller's coughing ...
    *(PEARCE arrives, in old tracksuit, basketball shoes.
    He remains about three days unshaven.)*
    Evening, Doctor Pearce.

PEARCE: Hello, Nancy. Still at it?

AUXILIARY: *(Leaving)* Cheeky.

PEARCE: *(To ANNA)* Hello.

ANNA: Hello.

PEARCE: There's been a bit of a balls-up.

ANNA: Really?

PEARCE: Yeah. Somebody should have told you to stop taking the Pill.

ANNA: Who, for instance?

PEARCE: *(Smiling)* Ah, well, there's some ... dispute about that. *(Pause)* Listen, we can't do a biopsy with that lot inside you. There's a risk of thrombosis ...

ANNA: Listen, I've been waiting nine weeks for this ...

PEARCE: I know. I'm sorry. Really.

ANNA: So how long will I have to wait?

PEARCE: It's not my case ... *(He stops himself, hating the words.)* You'll have to get back on cycle. We'll work it out and let you know ...

ANNA: Bloody hell.

PEARCE: *(Standing)* I'm sorry.

(PEARCE stands, moves fractionally towards CHRISTINE's bed.

CHRISTINE smiles at him shyly.

PEARCE crosses his fingers, smiles back at her, leaves. ANNA lies there for a while, then swings her feet on to the floor and pulls a long white paper carrier from under her bed, takes her clothes out, begins to get dressed.)

CHRISTINE: Anna? ...

(ANNA puts jeans on under nightdress.)

What're you doing?

ANNA: I'm off. No point staying here.

CHRISTINE: Did he say you could go? Shouldn't you ... see somebody?

ANNA: *(Clipping bra)* Yes. My feller. *(CHRISTINE watches her anxiously as she completes her dressing. Finally:)* Hey. Hope it goes Okay. See you.

(ANNA strides off down the darkened ward.

32

CHRISTINE watches her to the open doors leading past
the half-lit nurses' room, sees her path blocked by
the night sister and staff nurse.
Waves of verbal exchange meet her.
Finally ANNA strides off into the dark.
CHRISTINE turns to her locker, begins taking her pills.)
MRS SCULLY: What've they taken this time? Feels like half
   me insides. This is me third. Eeeh there'll be nowt
   left. The Queen Mother's had one, you know. And
   Petula Clark. Sister thing told me. Poor buggers.
   I hope they don't feel like me. *(Pause)* They made me
   sick, them crisps.

9. INT. WARD. NIGHT

CHRISTINE sleeps. Wakens suddenly.
The middle of the night. Low gasps and hisses from
SCULLY's bed area. She focuses on two young nurses who've
been changing her blood bag.
They talk in harsh whispers.
FIRST NURSE: Jesus Christ, look at it, it's all over ...
SECOND NURSE: Shh. Don't wake her for God's sake. She'll
   pull the place down. Take the bag, take the bag ...
FIRST NURSE: All right, I've got it.
   (They stare at each other, momentarily lost.)
   What are we going to *do*?
   (CHRISTINE edges forward, until she can see MRS SCULLY.
   Her face, hair, neck and pillows are splashed with
   blood from the bag the FIRST NURSE holds in her
   bloody hands.)
SECOND NURSE: You're a clumsy sod, I showed you how to do
   it.
FIRST NURSE: My hand slipped.
SECOND NURSE: My hand slipped. Sister'll love that.

(The FIRST NURSE sees CHRISTINE peering at them.)
FIRST NURSE: We'd better pull the curtains.
   (The curtains are drawn.
   CHRISTINE lies back, half hearing the muffled
   exchanges that persist.)
SECOND NURSE: Well, you'd better tell her. *(Pause)*
   Look at it!
   (Suddenly they're giggling, shushing each other.
   CHRISTINE turns over, returns to sleep.)

10. INT. WARD. DAY
ANAESTHETIST is preparing syringe and tray for injection.
ANAESTHETIST: *(OOV)* All right, Mrs Potts? This'll just
   make you feel nice and drowsy.
   (CHRISTINE sits propped in her bed, eyes quite heavy,
   but watching.
   CHATTERJEE has just finished taking MRS SCULLY's
   blood pressure, mutters 'Good Morning, Doctor' shyly,
   as SEAL arrives with a file.)
SEAL: Mrs Potts. All ready.
   (CHRISTINE smiles.)
   Now then, *(Sitting)* there's just another form here
   we'd like you to sign. Do you feel up to that?
CHRISTINE: What is it doctor?
SEAL: It's nothing to worry about. Mr Staunton thought
   it might be as well if you signed an open consent
   form too. Just in case.
   (Here show the modified consent form being held by
   DOCTOR SEAL. Casually pick out key words ... 'Frozen
   section (biopsy)? Proceed ? mastectomy'.)
   (Soothing VO) Then if there *were* anything, well, nasty,
   he could deal with it on the spot, instead of having
   to send you home and call you back again.

34

CHRISTINE: I see.

SEAL: Just there at the bottom. *(She guides CHRISTINE's signature.)* That's it. Good. *(She stands.)* See you in theatre, Mrs Potts.

(SEAL leaves.

CHRISTINE frowns a little, uneasy now.)

ANAESTHETIST: *(Who has been waiting)* Here we go then.

(Begins preparing the arm. CHRISTINE watches, fearful. ANAESTHETIST sees her, says, smiling:) No need to look, Mrs Potts.

(The ANAESTHETIST directs CHRISTINE's gaze away from the syringe. She looks at MRS SCULLY, scrubbed white again.)

MRS SCULLY: *(To no one)* I'm being buggered about.

(O'MALLEY and CHATTERJEE help CHRISTINE on to the theatre trolley. The PORTER stands by, blowing gum bubbles, in, out. O'MALLEY ties an ident-disc round CHRISTINE's left arm. CHATTERJEE places her file between her feet.)

O'MALLEY: All ready Mrs Potts. Have a good time.

(The PORTER trundles CHRISTINE up the ward.)

11. INT. CORRIDORS. DAY

We take CHRISTINE's trolley-view of the journey, through the ward, past WARREN's open door, out (on film) into the old tiled corridor. Past laundry, kitchens, clanging lift cages, X-ray (follow the white line), the inner semaphore of a Victorian general hospital.

12. INT. ANAESTHETIC ROOM. DAY

CHRISTINE lies, almost out, in pre-op. The ANAESTHETIST and his trainee talk OOV, as they give her a second injection. The trainee prepares the arm, but the assistant *gives the actual injection.*

ANAESTHETIST: Put it in the right, Charlie. Left breast,
    right arm, O.K.?

13. INT. OPERATING THEATRE. DAY

CHRISTINE is lifted onto operating table.
The REGISTRAR (George), SEAL, PEARCE, masked, stand
around waiting.

REGISTRAR: Any sign of Mr Staunton yet, sister?

THEATRE SISTER: On his way, Doctor Williams.

    (The REGISTRAR checks the time.)

    We're going to be pushed again ...

PEARCE: Why not go ahead?

    (The REGISTRAR stares at PEARCE for a long time, his
    eyes searching PEARCE's for some sign, a gleam of
    irony perhaps, that might save him from irredeemable
    certification. He finds nothing approaching it.)

REGISTRAR: *(Deliberately)* Doctor Pearce. I hope by the
    time you finish your training in this hospital you
    will have learnt the answer to that question.
    (CU clock above theatre door: 9.55. STAUNTON arrives,
    gowned, capped, but not gloved, glasses half-way down
    his nose. A chorus of good morning greets him. The
    THEATRE SISTER hands him the file, with bred deference.)

STAUNTON: Good morning. George. Doctor Seal. *(To SISTER:)*
    Thank you. Doctor Pearce. *(Quick look in file.)* Yes.
    Yes. Yes. Good, let's get started. *(To REGISTRAR:)*
    Off you go, doctor. We're waiting for you ...

14. INT. OPERATING THEATRE. DAY

CU the REGISTRAR working on the cut. CU STAUNTON, SEAL,
PEARCE. The REGISTRAR looks up at STAUNTON. They
exchange a longish look.

36

STAUNTON: Take it on a bit, George, mm?

    (CU REGISTRAR, returning to the cut.

    CU PEARCE, staring intently.

    The REGISTRAR looks across the table again at STAUNTON.)

    Do the section.

    (The REGISTRAR teases out a sliver of flesh, scraping

    it into a small round plastic container.)

REGISTRAR: *(OOV)* Path lab, nurse. Oh and phone

    Doctor Mount, tell him we might have something for his

    mice in an hour or so ...

    (CU CHRISTINE, in repose.)

STAUNTON: *(OOV)* How old is she?

    (Pan round table. Return to CU CHRISTINE. CU PEARCE.)

PEARCE: *(OOV)* Twenty-nine.

STAUNTON: *(OOV)* Twenty-nine.

REGISTRAR: *(OOV)* Any point waiting, do you think?

    (CU PEARCE.)

PEARCE: *(Half-muttering, barely audible)* We've waited

    three weeks, another 20 minutes won't make any

    difference ...

STAUNTON: Say something, Doctor Pearce?

PEARCE: *(Finally, looking away)* No.

15. INT. OPERATING THEATRE. DAY

CU file, containing Histologist's report on the section,
in the SISTER's hands while the REGISTRAR reads from it.
She then holds it for STAUNTON, who is now scrubbed-up
and gloved. He scans it briefly.

STAUNTON: Well, I suppose we knew as much. Let Doctor

    Seal and Doctor Pearce see it, will you Sister? Well,

    George, shall we have a look at the nodes ...

    (They close around the table.

    CU clock: 10.35.)

16. INT. OPERATING THEATRE. DAY

CU CHRISTINE's head in close up as she's wheeled out of
the theatre into the post-op area. Draw back to reveal
the process: the clock is at 12.40. Drip bottles -
saline only - attached. The doctors have retired to wash
up. Two nurses are cleaning the couch area, etc, another
lays out new instruments, etc.

17. INT. POST-OP. DAY

Post-op area. O'MALLEY stands a few paces away from
CHRISTINE's trolley, waiting for a porter.

O'MALLEY: *(To nurse passing through)* Did you see that
    porter feller anywhere?

    (Nurse shakes head, leaves.)

    He's an idle man.

    (CHRISTINE moans, stirs a little. O'MALLEY frowns,
    makes an impatient noise in her throat.)

18. INT. ANAESTHETIC ROOM. DAY

DOCTOR MOUNT, in a white coat, passes through the
anaesthetic room and raps on the theatre doors. The
THEATRE SISTER pokes her head out.

MOUNT: Doctor Mount. You've got some tissue for me.
SISTER: Yes, it's in the theatre, doctor. I'll just get
    it for you.

    (The SISTER disappears back into the theatre. MOUNT
    waits. She returns, and hands him a small round
    plastic lidded bowl containing tissue.)

    It's about fifty grammes. Will that be enough?
MOUNT: That's fine. Is that it?
SISTER: *(OOV)* That's it.
MOUNT: Frozen section say anything about the type?

    (PEARCE enters from the theatre.)

SISTER: Medullary, I think. I'll send a copy down, if
    you like.

MOUNT: Thanks.

> *(MOUNT talks on, though both grow aware of the silent,*
> *brooding figure at their side.)*

Medullary'll do nicely. *(Staring at tissue bowl.)* I'm
    trying implants on immune deprived mice.
    Subcutaneous. Intramuscular. Intravenous.
    Intrahepatic. If that goes well, I'll try a second
    passage of tumour solution by injection into the
    pleural and peritoneal cavities.

PEARCE: How long before you crack it then?

MOUNT: Hard to say. Believe it or not, a major problem
    is the shortage of tumour tissue.

PEARCE: *(Short, snapping laugh)* Yeah? Well, we'll have
    to see what we can do, won't we ...

> *(PEARCE leaves abruptly. SISTER coughs. MOUNT*
> *pockets his tissue.)*

MOUNT: I'd better get this to the fridge ...

SISTER: Odd to think of it ... living on like that.

MOUNT: Yes.

> *(MOUNT turns to go. As he does so another patient,*
> *out, is wheeled into the anaesthetic room, ready for*
> *the next operation.)*

19. INT. POST-OP. DAY

O'MALLEY and CHRISTINE still in post-op.

CU CHRISTINE, eyes open. A long moment.

CHRISTINE starting very low, a drunken mumble.

CHRISTINE: What have they done? What ...? What've
    they ...? *(Louder)* What have they done? What have
    they done?

O'MALLEY: Shh, you're all right, Mrs Potts ...

CHRISTINE: *(Louder)* What have they done? Eh? What have
they ...?

O'MALLEY: You're all right, Mrs Potts ... You've had
your operation and we're just waiting ...

CHRISTINE: *(Scream, harsh)* ... *What have they done to me?*

20. INT. WARD. NIGHT

*Ward 20. Evening, minutes before visitors. Tea things
are still being cleared, nurses finish off bed-rubs (soap
and powder) for the elderly frail. Everything that moves
creaks, rumbles, clanks; a second world war combat area.
CHRISTINE lies in her bed, propped, awake but sedated,
under her saline drip. Her face is very red, blotched
with crying. She stares up the ward at the ward doors,
which remain closed. The large puff bandage over her
left breast is slightly stained with blood.
SISTER WARREN emerges from the dayroom pushing a creaking
dirty linen skip before her. Surveys ward. Looks up at
clock: 7.40.*

WARREN: Let them in, nurse. We're ten minutes behind
again.

*(SEAL emerges from a curtained bed area, a nurse pulls
the curtains back.)*

SEAL: Give me a second or two will you, sister. I don't
want to get caught by the hordes ...

WARREN: Quick as you can then, doctor.

*(SEAL leaves up the ward. WARREN approaches SCULLY's
curtained bed area, peeps in.)*

Nearly finished, nurse?

O'MALLEY: Not really, sister.

*(O'MALLEY and CHATTERJEE are about to change SCULLY's
dressing.)*

WARREN: Quick as you can then. I'll get your temperatures

40

started for you ...

(WARREN recloses the curtain, moves on to CHRISTINE's
bed. Visitors surge in down the ward. CHRISTINE
watches them in a sort of dull anxiety.)

How are we feeling now, Mrs Potts?

CHRISTINE: *(Seeing her)* Sore.

WARREN: We'll give you something to help you sleep.

You'll feel better tomorrow.

(CHRISTINE returns to the visitors.)

I shouldn't be letting you have visitors, according
to regulations, Mrs Potts ...

(CHRISTINE looks at her again, some slight aggression
mounting in her.)

... Tell your husband to pop in on his way out, I'll
have a word with him, just to reassure him ...

(WARREN pushes the trolley off up the ward, passes JOE
on his way in, carrying a bunch of daffodils.

CHRISTINE sees him, begins to fill up and spill over.

He takes her hand nervously, anxious at once, ignoring
her tears, wishing them not there.)

JOE: I'm sorry I'm late, love. I went down the market
and got you these, we're working on Chaucer Street,
you know, the flats. *(Pause)* What you crying for?

CHRISTINE: They've taken it off, Joe.

(CHRISTINE tries to stem the flood of tears with a
Kleenex but it gets worse.

JOE can't find anything to say, in the shock and fear
of the moment.)

JOE: *(Finally)* I thought they were just doing tests, love.
(Pause) You weren't even ill. *(Looking round at the*
ward, embarrassed.) Listen, don't cry.

CHRISTINE: *(Working on her face with Kleenex)* I can't
help it. I'm sorry. *(She makes the effort.)* I'm ...

(She won't say it: 'frightened'.) I don't know why
they did it. Nobody's said.

JOE: I suppose they know best, Chris.

(MRS SCULLY screeches from her curtained bed area.)

SCULLY: Oh dear gentle Jesus they're killing me! God
Almighty don't, don't do that, oh, oh, oh, don't do
that, please, no, no, oh, oh ...

O'MALLEY: Nearly finished, Mrs Scully. We'll have you
right as rainwater in a tick, you see.

(The exchanges continue.

CHRISTINE stares ahead of her, deep in her fear.

*JOE stares at her in some desperation, anxious for
some word from her that will restore their normality
to them.)*

JOE: *(Finally)* What shall I do with the flowers?

CHRISTINE: Oh ... Take them up to the nurses' room,
they'll look after them ...

(JOE stands gratefully.)

Speak to the sister will you ... *(She's desperate.)*
Please.

JOE: *(Pinned again)* Do you think I should?

CHRISTINE: Please. *(Pause)* She said it'd be all right.

(JOE nods, leaves.

*CHATTERJEE unzips SCULLY's bed area, O'MALLEY pushes
the squeaky trolley with the soiled dressing into the
main aisle.)*

O'MALLEY: You're a brave lady, so you are, Mrs Scully.

(MRS SCULLY lies back, drained of all reply.

*The nurses move off up the ward through the glass
partition of the nurses' room. CHRISTINE can just
make out JOE talking to SISTER WARREN.)*

SCULLY: I've had it this time. I'll not see this through.

(CHRISTINE looks at her, hasn't even the energy to

42

> *console her. SCULLY's hands are on her midriff.)*
> There's nowt left. How'ma gonna get to the post
> office like this?
> *(CHRISTINE turns away, looks back up to the nurses'*
> *room.*
> *JOE leaves it, walks back into the ward and down to*
> *her bed.)*

JOE: *(Sitting down again)* I've seen her, love. She's
quite nice really.

CHRISTINE: What did she say?

JOE: Well, she said when they opened you up it were
pretty nasty and that there were some sort of
infection, so the specialist decided you'd be better
off without ...

> *(Pause)*

CHRISTINE: How long will I be in for, Joe?

JOE: Oh, she said about a fortnight. They have to do
some more tests and that.

> *(CHRISTINE has studied his face and manner for hints,*
> *clues to her condition, yet she's eager to take the*
> *hope offered.)*

CHRISTINE: Am I ... going to be all right?

JOE: Course you're gonna be all right. That's why they
did what they did. They're not fools, you know, these
people.

CHRISTINE: *(Bleak)* It's to be hoped to God they're not.

JOE: Hey, there's no point talking like that, our Chris.
You've got to start getting well again. You've got
two kiddies and a husband to look after.

> *(CHRISTINE begins to weep again, gently hopeless.)*

CHRISTINE: What am I going to do? Nothing'll fit me ...

JOE: Sister said they fix you up with something. *(Gentle,*
embarrassed, frightened by her unfamiliar despair.)

Hey. It'll be all right, chuck.

21. INT. WARD. NIGHT

Night. 2 a.m. by the ward clock. Old women cough, wheeze,
croak, ramble in their sleep.
Noise everywhere.
Track in on CHRISTINE, lying awake, staring at shadows.
After a moment, her right hand moves along the bedspread
until it contacts the vacated breast area.

22. INT. WARD. DAY

Morning, 10.15. Ward 20.
Staff nurse BRENTON hurries her nurses along, in
expectation of the consultant's weekly round.
BRENTON: Come along, Nurse Chatterjee. Let's get that
    finished, shall we.
    (CHATTERJEE shakes down a thermometer at MRS SCULLY's
    bed, enters temperature on chart, smooths the coverlet
    several times.)
CHATTERJEE: Just finished, Staff.
    (O'MALLEY comes into the ward.
    BRENTON turns to look at her.
    O'MALLEY nods, goes out again, enters nurses' room,
    where WARREN is adjusting her cap in a mirror. Some
    laughter at bottom of ward.)
BRENTON: All right, ladies. Settle down now. Mr Staunton
    is about to start his round and Mr Staunton likes a
    little quiet on the ward. *(She's turning, sees a*
    crushed grape on the floor, begins to tease it up with
    her finger, puts the skin into her pocket, borrows a
    Kleenex from a locker to wipe up the juice. To
    herself:) God Almighty, what do those cleaners *do!*
    (She's satisfied, strides off into the nurses' room.)

(CHRISTINE sits up in bed, still red, but rested.)

SCULLY: He's your man, inne, Staunton?

CHRISTINE: Yes.

SCULLY: I have Price. Had him for years. *(Pause)* Wait
    till I see him.

    *(The doors open and round begins, in all its rich and
    subtle ritual.*

    *STAUNTON has eleven patients in the ward, the first
    two up from CHRISTINE.*

    We take her POV as she sits and watches.

    *STAUNTON, George the REGISTRAR, SEAL and WARREN stand
    at the foot of the bed.*

    *WARREN hands STAUNTON file and bed-chart, says the
    patient's name clearly.*

    *The patient is not addressed. STAUNTON shows the
    REGISTRAR something in the file. Some brief, low
    discussion.*

    SEAL asks a question, almost unaudible.

    *WARREN answers, after hesitation. STAUNTON says
    something to SEAL which she writes up.*

    *They move to the foot of the next bed. Apart from a
    marginal (but still ineffective) increase in
    audibility, the procedure unfolds as before.*

    CU CHRISTINE, her face tensing as her turn approaches.

    They arrive at the bottom of her bed.)

WARREN: *(Handing file)* Mrs Potts, sir.

    *(STAUNTON half turns with the file, so that he's in
    less than half profile from the bed, as though shy or
    embarrassed. SEAL acknowledges CHRISTINE with a
    slight smile.*

    *The REGISTRAR asks a question of WARREN. All the
    exchanges are indistinct, barely audible, the odd word
    floating down the bed to CHRISTINE.*

45

Brackets indicate dimension of unclarity, for the
patient.)

REGISTRAR: (No problem with the) wound, sister?

WARREN: (None) at all, doctor.

SEAL: (Is she de)pressed, would you (say)?

WARREN: (Just a bit) down, doctor. (It's only) natural,
I (sup)pose.

REGISTRAR: (What about the) radivac?

SEAL: (About a) hundred c.c.s.

(STAUNTON says something wholly inaudible, his back
almost wholly turned to CHRISTINE.
The REGISTRAR looks up the bed at her, studies her
for a moment.)

REGISTRAR: *(Audibly)* Possibly. What do you suggest, sir?

(STAUNTON replies after a moment, again wholly
inaudibly.
The REGISTRAR speaks to WARREN, who nods.
They move on, in order, beyond MRS SCULLY's bed,
towards the bottom of the ward.)

WARREN: *(Cheerfully)* Thank you, Mrs Potts. *(She joins the*
doctors.)

SCULLY: *(Racking whisper)* Doesn't he look like Prince
Philip! He's going bald you know. Spent thousands
on hair restorer. I read it in the *People*.

WARREN: *(Up the ward)* Thank you Mrs Scully!

(MRS SCULLY deliberates a reply for a moment, then
reaches for her plastic water jug and glass. Her
frail hand sets up a rattling in the sepulchral
quiet of the ward.
She winks at CHRISTINE; wicked. The water begins to
splash over the locker.
WARREN gestures to a standing nurse at the top of the
ward. The nurse, O'MALLEY,approaches MRS SCULLY's bed

46

        area, takes the jug off her.)

O'MALLEY: *(Sotto voce)* You're nothing but a little girl,
        Mrs Scully. What are you?

        (MRS SCULLY stares at her.)

SCULLY: *(Finally)* Thirsty. It's like the bloody desert,
        this place, it's so full of dust.

O'MALLEY: *(Minatory, mopping floor with Kleenex)* That'll
        do you now, Mrs Scully.

23. INT. WARD. DAY

*Afternoon, towards 3 p.m. The ward rests desultorily,
thin sunlight washing the floors.*

*Ambulants gather in clusters about beds. The woman with
the Zimmer-frame wanders from bed to bed, trying to cadge
some Lucozade. The PORTER and BRENTON are wheeling in
the last of the day's theatre patients, restoring her to
her bed. The trolley-shop works its way down the ward.
CHRISTINE's bed area is curtained.*

*Inside, CHATTERJEE has just begun dressing the wound.
CHRISTINE lies half on her back, her head averted, her
left arm extended only slightly, but enough to give her
pain.*

CHATTERJEE: Will it go any further, Mrs Potts?

        (CHRISTINE shakes her head.)

        Come on, I'm sure it will, just a weeny bit more ...

        (CHRISTINE closes her eyes on the new pain.)

        ... That's it ... There. I'll try not to hurt
        you ... *(She begins removing puff-bandage dressing
        with textbook devotion. Lifts the final dressing.
        Examines the wound.)* That's an excellent wound,
        Mrs Potts.

        *(CHATTERJEE looks at CHRISTINE, who tacitly but
        unequivocally refuses the oblique invitation to look.*

She begins to clean it, doing her throttled best.)
You know, they say Mr Staunton's the best surgeon in
the hospital. Sister told me he could have been in
Harley Street ... You were lucky to get him,
really ... Good stitches. Excellent. *(She works on,
eyeing CHRISTINE's still averted face from time to
time.)* Your husband can bring your children in on
Sunday. They'll cheer you up ... *(She works on
finally.)* I'm applying the new dressing now, Mrs
Potts. *(She waits. CHRISTINE makes no response.)*
All right? *(She begins the new application.)*
(BRENTON's voice from ward.)

BRENTON: *(OOV)* Nurse Chatterjee.

CHATTERJEE: Here, staff.

(BRENTON's head pokes in.)

BRENTON: Lend a hand with Buckley, she's back from
theatre.

CHATTERJEE: Nearly finished, staff.

BRENTON: Have you seen O'Malley?

CHATTERJEE: No, staff.

*(BRENTON withdraws. CHATTERJEE begins taping the
bandage. CHRISTINE turns at last, to look at it.)*
That wasn't so bad, was it.

CHRISTINE: Thank you.

*(CHATTERJEE stands, begins to reorganise her trolley.
Begins to unzip the curtains.)*
Nurse, do you think I could have a word with sister?

CHATTERJEE: *(Turning)* What is it, Mrs Potts?

CHRISTINE: It's nothing. I just wanted a word with her.

CHATTERJEE: *(Finishing curtains)* I'll see if she's free.
All right?

CHRISTINE: Thank you.

(WARREN moves down the ward, eyes flicking from side

to side. She straightens a couple of visitors' chairs,
adjusts some tulips in a vase, picks something up from
the floor and pockets it, arrives at CHRISTINE's bed.)

WARREN: Hello, Mrs Potts. What can we do for you?

CHRISTINE: *(Low voice)* I think I've started my period,
sister. It shouldn't be till next week, I'm usually
very regular ...

WARREN: Not to worry. It does happen sometimes ... I'll
get you some tampons. All right?

CHRISTINE: Do you think I might have a bath, sister?

WARREN: It's all right, Mrs Potts, we'll clean you up.
I'll send a nurse down, we can't have that wound
getting wet ...

CHRISTINE: Couldn't I have a bath, sister?

WARREN: *(Thinking a moment)* Well, we'd have to be
careful.

(Pause. CHRISTINE pleads silently.)

I'll see what we can do ... All right?

CHRISTINE: Thank you, sister.

WARREN: *(Leaving)* Any time.

24. INT. TOILET AREA. DAY

Bath filling with hot water. O'MALLEY tests the water,
turns off the taps, moves out of the bathroom into the
general toilet area, where CHRISTINE sits, in bathrobe,
in wheelchair.

A frail, elderly woman comes in, goes into a lavatory
cubicle, closes the door.

O'MALLEY: Here we go then.

(O'MALLEY pushes CHRISTINE into the bathroom, begins
to help her to her feet.)

Now for God's sake don't let us get that wound wet
or you'll have me shot.

(O'MALLEY's massive arms support CHRISTINE as she
sinks into the water. CHRISTINE sits facing the door.)
How is it? Not too hot?

CHRISTINE: It's lovely.

O'MALLEY: Don't splash.
(A loudish cry of 'shit!' from the cubicle across the
room.)
Oh God, that sounds like Mrs Goodwin's Translet gone
for a burton again ...
(O'MALLEY leaves the bathroom, the door stays open
behind her, crosses to the cubicle. CHRISTINE watches
her.)
Mrs Goodwin, are you all right?

GOODWIN: *(Behind door)* It's my bag. I dropped it getting
it off.

O'MALLEY: Let's have a look. You should have emptied
that hours ago.

GOODWIN: I couldn't get if off ...

O'MALLEY: I showed you myself how to take it off ...

GOODWIN: It wouldn't come off, it doesn't fit
properly ...

O'MALLEY: Wait there. Don't move.
(O'MALLEY goes out, clucking. CHRISTINE stares
through the two open doors at the seated woman, who
sits vacantly for a while before becoming aware of
her.)

GOODWIN: It's a bugger, innit. *(Pause)* She didn't show
me how to do it, you know. Two minutes she spent.
(Pause) What's up wi' you?

CHRISTINE: Breast.

GOODWIN: Oh. *(Sniffs)* What a caper. I'll be well shut
of this place. I will.
(CHRISTINE withdraws into her bathing. GOODWIN goes

on muttering to herself. O'MALLEY returns with LUCY,
the cleaner. LUCY looks at the bag.)

LUCY: Here, I'm supposed to be on 18 now. Are you sure
sister's talked to Mrs Prince?

O'MALLEY: Lucy, it'll only take you a minute ...

LUCY: I'd better see sister. It's more than my job's
worth ... If the Organiser says so, that's a
different matter. Ward 18's where I'm supposed to
be ...

(LUCY leaves. O'MALLEY follows her.
Another patient comes in, about thirty, looks at
GOODWIN. GOODWIN pushes the door to aggressively with
her hand. The patient pulls a face, changes her mind,
walks out.
CHRISTINE tries to wash her legs with her right hand,
the left one, bent at the elbow to clear the water,
pretty well unusable.)

25. INT. WARD. DAY

CHRISTINE sits on her bed, an unopened copy of the Sun
on her thighs.

A religious visitor makes his way down the ward, placing
a four-page leaflet on every bed and uttering magic
formulas to their occupants. He reaches CHRISTINE.

VISITOR: *(Short, bald, about forty-five)* Good news,
sister.

(CHRISTINE looks for it.)

The Lord Christ is risen. And the Lord Christ loves
you. *(He hands CHRISTINE the pamphlet.)* Read the
Lord's Word. For the Lord will make you whole.
(He smiles, inconsequentially, passes on to SCULLY.)
Good news, sister.

SCULLY: What's that then?

VISITOR: The Lord Christ is risen.

SCULLY: I should hope he is, it's bloody teatime.   Is
   he on nights then?

VISITOR: And the Lord Christ loves you.

SCULLY: That's nice.

VISITOR: *(Handing her pamphlet)*   Read the Lord's Word.
   For the Lord will make you whole.

SCULLY: Gonna get me foot back, then, am I?   And me
   bowels?

VISITOR: *(Unnerved)* Have faith, sister.   Faith can move
   mountains.

SCULLY: I bet it can't move this place.

VISITOR: Read the Lord's Word ... *(He's leaving, the
   same irrelevant smile forming.)*

SCULLY: Piss off. I'm a Catholic.

   *(The VISITOR proceeds down the ward, restoring his
   ritual.*

   *CHRISTINE flicks the pages of the pamphlet, which is
   laid out in question and answer format, with clinching
   quotes from the New Testament in heavy type.)*

   I could fancy a drink of someat.

CHRISTINE: I've got some lemon squash.

SCULLY: You haven't a drop of gin, have you? No, I
   thought not. I like a drop of gin.

   (CHRISTINE looks at the Sun. *She must have seen the
   front page twenty times. Opens it. On page 3 half
   page, a nude dolly, both stunning breasts on display.
   She closes it again. SEAL arrives.)*

SEAL: *(Checking watch)*   Thought I'd just drop in before
   visitors, Mrs Potts. How are you? *(She looks at
   charts at bottom of bed.)*

CHRISTINE: A bit better, doctor.

SEAL: Good, good. The physiotherapist will probably call

tomorrow, get that arm of yours moving. If things go
well, we'll have the first lot of stitches out within
the week.

(Pause. Looking at file.)

CHRISTINE: Yes, doctor.

SEAL: That's all right. Perfectly normal. Nothing to
worry about.

CHRISTINE: *(Tentative)* Everybody looked ... very
serious, this morning, doctor ...

SEAL: Serious? No, no. *(Pause)* Mr Staunton does a very
formal round. He's of the old school you know. But
you're in good hands.

CHRISTINE: He didn't seem to want to ... look at me,
doctor.

SEAL: You mustn't imagine things, Mrs Potts. He's
always pressed, that's all ... He's done all that's
needed. Now we just wait until you're well enough
to go home. Mr Williams the Registrar will probably
want a word with you early next week, when the results
of the tests are through ...

CHRISTINE: Tests?

SEAL: Nothing to concern yourself over, they're just
routine tests we carry out in cases like yours. *(She
looks at watch.)* Good. Your iron pills aren't
giving you trouble are they?

CHRISTINE: No, I don't think so, doctor.

SEAL: Good. Good.

CHRISTINE: What happened to that young one?

(SEAL frowns, not understanding.)

With the hair ...

SEAL: Doctor Pearce. I think it's his day off. Did you
want something?

CHRISTINE: No. *(Pause)* I just wondered.

SEAL: *(Watch again)* Well, I'll look in tomorrow. Keep
     smiling.
     (SEAL off up the ward. As she reaches the far doors,
     BRENTON begins locking them back to admit evening
     visitors.
     SEAL wades through the 'waves of the great unwashed',
     her expressionless gaze fixed on the corridor.
     We follow a short, sturdy, grey-haired woman of fifty-
     five back down the ward. She wears a bottle-green
     longish coat, flat shoes, a handbag, frowns as she
     searches for the bed. Sees CHRISTINE eventually,
     moves towards her.)
WOMAN: There you are. *(Bending, to kiss CHRISTINE's hair.)*
     Thought I'd got the wrong ward. How are you, lass?
CHRISTINE: Hello, mum. *(She reaches for a Kleenex, begins*
     to blow her nose, her eyes leaking again.)
WOMAN: *(Sitting)* Let's have a look at you.

26. INT. WARD. NIGHT

Ward 20. Beyond midnight. A woman coughs and coughs,
remorselessly, at the bottom of the ward.
SCULLY snores and snorts.
Beds creak. Moans. Occasional sleep calls.
CHRISTINE lies wide-eyed, her fingers beating time to
the woman coughing. She peers up the ward at the lit
nurses' room. Looks back at the ceiling. CU. Fear and
tension growing, an unresolved dialogue somewhere inside
her head. She shakes her head several times, answering
herself.
She sits up, watches the ward: drips, bottles, trolleys,
lockers, sleeping heads, then white hair, scrawny,
arthritic arms on counterpanes.
Listens. A crash from the day room, unexplained,

54

unnoticed, unaccounted for.

Slowly, she pushes her feet to the floor, feels for her
fluffy slippers in the locker, drops them between her legs,
houses her feet in them, unhooks her dressing gown,
stands waveringly to put it on.

She holds her left arm in a hard defensive curve. Looks
at clock: 12.55. Begins to walk, with infinite care, up
the ward.

She reaches the ward doors that lead to toilets on left
and nurses' room on right. Leans her right side on flap
to open a wing, shuffles through.

27. INT. CORRIDOR. NIGHT

CHRISTINE stands for a moment, only feet from the night
sister and two nurses who sit in the nurses' room. Walks
past the door unseen and into the toilet area, now only
dimly lit.

28. INT. TOILET AREA. NIGHT

CHRISTINE closes the door behind her, clicks on a switch,
which lights the bathrooms, clicks it off, clicks on the
lights over the two lavatory cubicles, moves towards the
first one - occupied that afternoon by MRS GOODWIN.

She turns into the other cubicle. Locks the door. Sits
heavily, exhausted, on the closed lavatory seat, stares at
the dull green door.

29. INT. ENTRANCE HALL. NIGHT

Vestibule, block entrance, poorly lit.

PEARCE goes very slowly round and round in the swing
doors. He wears an old broad stripe double-breasted
Italian suit, an anonymous old trilby, three days' stubble,
shiny pointed Italian shoes, dirty white mac over his

shoulder. He's had a fair few, is gently slewed. As he
creaks round, he sings contralto to himself.
PEARCE: When you walk through the storm keep your head
up high and don't be afraid of the dark ...
(The clock over the door says 1.30.)

30. INT. WARD. NIGHT

Ward 20. A STAFF NURSE and a STUDENT NURSE do the hourly
round. They're three beds up from CHRISTINE's; the STAFF
NURSE shines a torch on to MRS GOODWIN's face.
STAFF NURSE: Thank God she's sleeping ... Did you hear
about her this afternoon ...?
NURSE: In the lavatories, you mean?
STAFF NURSE: Keep an eye on her tomorrow morning, that's
all.
(Torch out, they move on to next bed, flash light on
sleeping face, study it a moment, listening, light
out, move on, flash light on ANNA's empty bed.)
(Disgusted) Look at that. That's that student, you
know. Wasted. A whole week. With people clamouring
to get in.

31. INT. VISITORS' TOILETS. NIGHT

Inside, PEARCE switches on the lights in the tiny,
two-stone room; is immediately assailed by the stench;
looks down at the floor, half-flooded with stagnant
urine and water. Paper and other rubbish fill the drain
channel. The stones are urine-stained, dark brown and
yellow. He wades to the nearest stone, prepares to piss.
PEARCE: *(To wall)* No, it's not the consultants' day room
your worship, it's the male visitors' lavatory.
Regal, sir, wonderful choice of word if I may say so.
Fit for a king. Preferably a king in his wellies.

What was that sir? Seafresh, we call it. Ozone.
Delightful isn't it. Well sir, you know our motto
here at St Luke's - 'Es bildet ein Talent sich in der
Stille, Sich ein Charakter in dem Strom der Welt.'
'Genius is formed in quiet, character in the *stream*
of human life.' *(Pause)* Naturlich.

32.   INT.   TOILET AREA.   NIGHT

CHRISTINE sits in the lavatory, hugging herself, face
white.   Knocking on the door.   CHRISTINE ignores it; sits
on, impassive.

STAFF NURSE: *(OOV)* Come along, Mrs Potts. I know you're
    there. *(Knocks again.)* This is ridiculous, come along
    now.

    (Sounds of others entering.)

    She's in here, sister. The Lord knows how long she's
    been here ...

SISTER: *(OOV)* Is she all right?

STAFF NURSE: *(OOV)* I don't know. She won't answer me.

SISTER: *(OOV. Gently)* Mrs Potts. Mrs Potts. It's
    Sister. Open the door.

CHRISTINE: I'm all right. Leave me alone.

SISTER: *(OOV)* You can't sit in there all night, Mrs Potts.
    What is it? Come on, you can tell me.

    (CHRISTINE's face sets. Silence.)

    (OOV) Mrs Potts. Mrs Potts. *(Nothing)* All right,
    we'll have to get you out.

    (The SISTER begins giving instructions.

    CHRISTINE looks up to the top of the cubicle. Crane
    up to take the reverse shot: CHRISTINE looking up on
    one side, the SISTER giving instructions on the other.)

    (To STUDENT NURSE) ... You'll find a ladder in the
    kitchens, I think. Staff, you'd better help, no,

better still, keep an eye open for Senior Sister March
- we could do without her for the next ten minutes ...
*(They leave, the junior nurses in a hurry. The SISTER
turns in the doorway.)*
This is very childish, Mrs Potts. And you a mother ...
with two growing girls ...
*(The SISTER waits for some response. In the cubicle,
CHRISTINE stands, puts her hand on the bolt, withdraws
it again as the door closes behind the SISTER.)*

33. INT. CORRIDOR. NIGHT

*PEARCE wanders along another corridor, his coat collar
turned up, mac over shoulder, trilby pulled down over
eyes: a regular Philip Marlowe. He feels in his pocket
for a Camel, flicks one clumsily but effortlessly up into
his nostril, makes the necessary adjustment, fails to get
his throwaway briquet to work.*
*The STUDENT NURSE comes out of the kitchens behind him
carrying the steps. She looks at him warily.*
PEARCE: I should put some nail varnish on that, nurse.
    Stop it running. Here, let me have that.
    *(PEARCE goes to take it from the STUDENT NURSE. She
    frowns.)*
    It's all right, I'm a doctor. Aye, well, takes all
    sorts ... *(He fumbles his plastic ident card from his
    top pocket.)* See ... doctor. All right? *(He takes
    the ladder.)* Where do you want it?
NURSE: Ward 20, doctor. Women's Surgical.
PEARCE: Right.
    (PEARCE hunks it off. The STUDENT NURSE follows.)
    Admitted a giant have we?
    *(The STUDENT NURSE looks at PEARCE, he looks at the
    ladder.)*

NURSE: Oh. No, a patient's locked herself in the
     lavatory.

PEARCE: While the balance of mind was disturbed,
     presumably?

     (They reach the doors. The STUDENT NURSE holds them
     open for PEARCE. He's confronted by the NIGHT SISTER
     and the STAFF NURSE.)

     I was passing. Can I help?

SISTER: *(Doubtful)* Well, I think we can handle it,
     Doctor Pearce ...

PEARCE: I'd like to, if that's all right ... Who is it?

SISTER: Mrs Potts in 8. She had a radical two days ago.
     (PEARCE nods he knows.)
     She's been in for an hour, I estimate. She won't say
     why, won't come out.
     (PEARCE thinks for a moment. Very serious.)

PEARCE: Let me see what I can do. OK? Is there a
     wheelchair about?

34. INT. TOILET AREA. NIGHT

Inside the cubicle. CHRISTINE has resumed her seat.
Sounds outside. PEARCE's head appears above the door.

PEARCE: *(Perfect Bogart)* Here's looking at you, kid.
     (CHRISTINE looks at him. PEARCE tics his lips across
     his teeth, Bogart to the inch.)
     Listen, sweetheart, we gotta stop meeting like this.
     (CHRISTINE laughs.)
     No foolin' honey, this ain't no ladder of fame I'm
     currently negotiatin' ... believe me ...

CHRISTINE: What do you want?

PEARCE: *(Own voice)* I've lost an 8s needle, I wondered
     if you'd seen it. What do you think I want, you
     daft haporth, open the door.

(CHRISTINE doesn't move.)

Come on, I can't stop up here all night. It's
undignified, a man in my position. What do you think
Staunton'd say if he were to walk in now?
(CHRISTINE laughs again.)

It's all right laughing, you could be witnessing the
termination of a thoroughly promising career ...
*(He appears to slip, manages somehow to hang on, pulls
himself up, turns into Norman Evans, massages his left
breast with pain-clenched face.)* Ooh, that's the third
time today on the same wun, I'll cut his breath off,
the little bugger ... *(CHRISTINE laughs again.)*

I'm getting down now. All right?
*(Toilet area. PEARCE reaches the floor, moves the
ladder. Watches the door. Eventually it opens.
CHRISTINE stands in the doorway.)*

Hi.

CHRISTINE: Hello.

PEARCE: Fancy a cocoa?

CHRISTINE: How?

PEARCE: Come on.

*(PEARCE takes CHRISTINE's arm, leads her out past the
collected nurses, winks at the SISTER, sits
CHRISTINE in the chair, pushes her out into the
corridor.)*

35.   INT.   CORRIDOR.   NIGHT

PEARCE: *(Over shoulder)* Won't be long, sister. Just
having a cocoa.

36.   PEARCE'S ROOM.   NIGHT

*PEARCE's cramped, untidy room, lit by fierce but local
anglepoises on floor, desk and shelf.*

Work litters most surfaces. He pours hot milk into two
cups of cocoa, stirs, sugars, carries them to where
CHRISTINE sits in her wheelchair.
He still wears his clothes as before, though he's dropped
the mac.

CHRISTINE: I suppose you think I've ... gorra screw loose
or someat.

PEARCE: *(Cocoa up; toast)* Here's looking at you, kid.
(CHRISTINE smiles, looks down into her cup to taste
it. Is suddenly overcome by it all, fatigued,
desperate, very low.
PEARCE sits down opposite her in a mothy old armchair,
half disappearing in it.)
We could have some music, but my violin's at the
menders.
(CHRISTINE stares on at the cocoa, miserable, not
looking at PEARCE.)
I don't want to ask what it is, because I *know*, and
it's a sort of impotence, knowing what causes someone
grief and not being able to do anything about it.

CHRISTINE: *(Small voice)* I just want to get better.

PEARCE: Yeah.

CHRISTINE: Nobody says anything. They treat you as if
you were already dead. The specialist, he never even
looked at me, let alone spoke. *(Long pause.)* I know it
were serious. I'm not a child. You don't cut a thing
like that off for nothing. *(Long pause.)* I don't want
... fobbing off. *(Pause)* I don't know, maybe I'm being
... stupid. *They* know what they're doing, that's what
me husband says, that's what me mother says ... Just
... let 'em gerron with it ... don't be stupid ...
(CHRISTINE looks at PEARCE suddenly. He takes the
look, sunk in his chair.)

I just want to get better. *(Pause)* But I want to know what I'm facing.

PEARCE: I'm ... not in charge of your case, you know that don't you? I'm a trainee.

(CHRISTINE draws back in her chair, sensing another evasion.)

I'll tell you what I know. Which is most of what there is to know. The lump in your breast was a malignant tumour. A cancer.

(CHRISTINE swallows, looks back at her mug of cocoa, faint with fear yet oddly relieved.)

Can I go on?

(CHRISTINE nods once.)

We couldn't have known it, not your own doctor, not us in out-patients; a hundred thousand and more breast lumps are seen every year and very very few are malignant like yours. Particularly at your age. Equally, you did everything you should have done. As soon as you spotted it, you told your G.P. Your G.P. informed the hospital. The hospital sent for you as soon as it could. *(Pause)* Three weeks later. You were a low-cancer risk, marked non-urgent. We were wrong, but we weren't to blame. Yet, if there hadn't been 600,000 people competing for 500,000 hospital beds, we'd have seen you within a fortnight, and maybe taken it out before it had a chance to move. You know, even when it is cancer, we don't always have to remove the breast. *(Pause)* Well, it did move. At any rate, we found traces of it in some lymph nodes under the arm ... sort of glands ... So we took those out too. *(Pause)* As far as we know we've cleared the site. But just to make sure, when the stitches are out and the wound's healed, it's

possible we'll treat the whole area with radiation
- it isn't very pleasant, but it might be worth it.
(Pause) It's ... hard to explain why you haven't been
told all this, why we go on talking about this
'infection' and 'nasty tissue' ... I mean, there are
a thousand reasons, most of them decent and
honourable. Mainly, I think, it's because we have
lost all idea of you as a whole, human being, with a
past, a personality, dependents, needs, hopes, wishes.
Our power is strongest when you are dependent upon
it. We invite you to behave as the sum of your
symptoms. And on the whole you are pleased to oblige.
(Long pause.) Mr Staunton's a good man. He's
just ... not used, not equipped ... to deal with you
as a person. The gap is too great. *(Pause)* And
there's something else. The reason he can't speak to
you, look at you, after the operation is that for him
you represent a failure, even when the operation is a
success. Because each time we use surgery we fail,
medicine fails, the system fails, and he knows it,
and he bears the guilt. He really can't bear to see
what he's done to you, Mrs Potts. It makes him feel
crude ... and insensitive ... and ignorant in the real
sense; without knowledge. But if he can't face the
inadequacies of his profession, who else is allowed
to? The junior doctors, struggling to become
consultants? The nurses, struggling to make sense of
the mad world they've inherited? ... *(Very long
pause.)* In spite of which ... you're better off now
than you would have been if you hadn't come forward
for screening. *(He stops. Sits up, leans forward.)*
Listen. The father of medicine was a man called
Hippocrates. Two and a half thousand years ago he

said something we've forgotten. He said: 'Whoever
treats of this art should treat of things which are
familiar to the common people. For of nothing else
will such a one have to inquire or treat, but of the
diseases under which the common people have laboured,
which diseases and the causes of their origin and
departure, their increase and decline, unlettered
persons cannot easily find out for themselves, but
still it is easy for them to understand these things
when discovered and expounded by others ... For
whoever does not reach the capacity of the common
people and fails to make them listen to him, misses
his mark.' Well, we're all missing the mark,
Mrs Potts. And we need to be told. Not just
doctors and nurses, but administrators and office men
and boards of management and civil servants and
politicians and the whole dank crew that sail this
miserable craft through the night. *(Long silence. His
cocoa's cold. He puts it down.)* Do you know something?
My mother's proud of me. *(He laughs drily.)* Wow ...
(Another silence.)

CHRISTINE: Thank you.

PEARCE: Don't thank. Demand.

CHRISTINE: *(Slowly)* What are the chances ...?

PEARCE: Your chances are good, Mrs Potts. We'll know
how good when we've seen the full results of the
tests. But they're good. But from now on, you live
every day for keeps. The rest of us may continue to
cherish the illusion that we're immortal. You know
you're not. *(He stands, smiles at CHRISTINE.)* I'll
probably get sacked for this. Unethical behaviour.
(Pause) I wouldn't mind, but I hardly laid a hand on
you.

(CHRISTINE blushes a little, laughing with pleasure.
PEARCE leans across the wheelchair, looks into her
eyes.)

Here's looking at you, kid.

37. INT. WARD. DAY

Ward 20. CHRISTINE lies in her bed, having alternate
stitches removed by CHATTERJEE. She observes the
procedure in silence, but very carefully.
The scar, still very red, runs from deep armpit to
sternum in a long bent diagonal. At the bottom, a rubber
drain is sunk under the skin.
CHATTERJEE raises the knot of each stitch, snips it on
the clean side and pulls the clean side through the skin.
When she's finished the stitches, CHATTERJEE carefully
lifts the drain out. Swabs the wound with sterile water.
Prepares a small dressing.
CHRISTINE looks at the cut critically.

CHRISTINE: It's a mess.

CHATTERJEE: It's a beautiful scar.

CHRISTINE: What did he do it with, a bottle.

      (CHRISTINE grins at CHATTERJEE, ribbing her.
      CHATTERJEE relaxes, applies the dressing. Packs her
      trolley. Unzips the curtains.)

CHATTERJEE: I'll be glad to see the last of you,
      Mrs Potts.

      (CHRISTINE smiles, lies back.

      ANNA JAY leans across from the next bed.)

ANNA: Hi.

CHRISTINE: Hello. You're back then.

ANNA: (Cautious) Couldn't keep me away. Thought you'd've
      gone.

CHRISTINE: So did I. (She undoes her nightdress, shows

ANNA *the dressing.)* They took it all.

ANNA: *(Closing eyes)* Oh God. I'm sorry ...

CHRISTINE: Yes. *(Pause)* Can't be helped.

   (Pause. ANNA's very tense.)

   Where there's life, eh?

   (Pause. ANNA offers CHRISTINE some fruit.)

   When do you go?

ANNA: Day after tomorrow, I think.

CHRISTINE: You'll be all right. *(She eats a grape.)*

38. INT. WARD. NIGHT

CHRISTINE sleeps. ANNA stands over her, on SCULLY's
side, blows on her face to waken her. She wakens slowly.

ANNA: *(Whispering)* Shh. Mrs Scully's having a drink-up.

   She's going home tomorrow, she says.

CHRISTINE: What? She's not going home tomorrow ...

ANNA: Well, she wants you to say goodbye ... Bring

   your glass.

CHRISTINE: *(Chuckling)* She's batty. *(Getting out of bed.)*

   Let's have a look.

   (A door closes at top of ward. They stare up it,
   towards nurses' room.

   In it, SISTER writes up unending notes; two nurses
   play liar dice.

   They let themselves into MRS SCULLY's curtained bed
   area with silent stealth.

   MRS SCULLY plays hostess, pouring from a large
   lemonade bottle. Three other patients in the
   drink-up. MRS SCULLY beams wickedly at CHRISTINE.)

SCULLY: Give us your glass. Gin. Our Ethel brought it,

   bless her. Come on ... *(She pours a large helping.)*

   There y'are ... How're you ladies, all right are you?

   A toast. *(She looks round.)*

(The nurses' hands shield the throw: three queens.)

CHRISTINE: You're never going home tomorrow ...

SCULLY: I know. Sod it.

*(MRS SCULLY drinks. Looks at ANNA owlishly. ANNA
raises her glass.)*

ANNA: *(Repeating toast)* Sod it. *(She looks at CHRISTINE.)*

CHRISTINE: *(Grinning)* Sod it.

*(The other three whisper 'fuck it' in unison. They
begin to laugh as they drink.*

Shot of the curtained cubicle from the aisle.

Suppressed snorts of laughter.

Fade out.)

SUCH IMPOSSIBILITIES

CHARACTERS

TOM MANN

SHIP'S DOCTOR

SHIP'S OFFICER

SEAMAN

GERARD GROARK, Steward, Maritime Hall

NIGHT PORTER

JAMES FRANK PEARCE, Secretary, Ship Stewards' Union

TERENCE DIXON, Secretary, Seamen and Fireman's Union

THOMAS DITCHFIELD, Secretary, Mersey Quay and Railway
  Carters' Union

BILLAL QUILLIAM, Solicitor, Mersey Quay and Railway
  Carters' Union

JAMES SEXTON, Secretary, National Union of Dock
  Labourers; magistrate

MARTHA CLARKE, stenographer

MILLIGAN, Secretary, No 12 Branch, Dockers' Union

CUTHBERT LAWS, General Manager, Shipping Federation

POLICE SUPERINTENDENT

HEAD CONSTABLE

LORD MAYOR OF LIVERPOOL

MONTAGUE

CARRINGTON General Managers, shipping lines

MENTEITH

ELLEN MANN

SAWYER

DOCKERS

SEAMEN

ARMY

POLICE

1. FILM. 5.30 A.M. LIME STREET STATION

A swathe of steam clears around TOM MANN, grip on
platform, a small notebook in his hand. He consults it
briefly, picks up the grip, walks towards the barrier.
He's short, stockily built, lithe and powerful; a very
young fifty-odd. His thick hair is only slightly grey;
his full walrus moustache good and black. He wears a
good serge three-piece; a watch-chain across his middle.
(Song: 'Rise Up Jock' (Bob and Carole Pegg) begins.)

2. LIME STREET APPROACH

It's a bright day. At this time, the city is quiet, save
for an odd delivery cart here and there. MANN strides
down the approach, comes out by St George's Hall, stops
to watch a cavalry detachment pass at the canter.
(Song - second verse: 'O the first come was a Soldier'.)

3. PRINCE'S DOCK. SIGNING-ON HALL OF THE WHITE STAR
LINE, INCORPORATED MEMBER OF THE SHIPPING FEDERATION

A knot of SEAMEN stand by the entrance to the great
draughty shed. MANN stops to talk with them. (Song
- third verse: 'And the next come was a Sailor'.)
SEAMAN hands MANN a white card - his Shipping Federation
ticket - and MANN continues in. (Song ends on third
chorus of 'Rise Up Jock'.)

4. INT. THE HALL

Long straggles of SEAMEN attend the eight or ten
inspection and call-in tables scattered throughout it.

The men wear only trousers, carry boots, socks, shirts,
coats and hats in their hands. At each desk, a medical
supervisor and a Line official. MANN stands, observes,
grip in hand. A Line OFFICIAL approaches.

OFFICIAL: You for calling?

MANN: That's right.

OFFICIAL: You'd better get in line then. You won't do
    yourself much good standing there.

    (The OFFICIAL moves off. MANN slowly joins a queue.
    Ahead of him, the SEAMAN at the table is removing his
    trousers. The MEDICAL SUPERVISOR, who remains
    seated, motions him to turn round and bend over, then
    parts his buttocks with a ferrule and briefly inspects
    his anus. The man then turns round, has his legs
    parted by the ferrule and his penis raised. All this
    time, he tries to keep a hold on his clothing.
    Finally, he presents his ticket (held between his
    teeth) and signs on. All round the hall, variations
    on this simple, brutal procedure can be observed.
    Finally, MANN reaches the table.)

    What's wrong with you then?

MANN: Nothing. How do you mean?

OFFICIAL: Clothes, man, clothes. What do you think
    you're playing at. We haven't got all day, you know.

    (Pause. Looking hard.) You got a ticket?

MANN: Yes.

OFFICIAL: Let's have it then.

    (MANN hands it over. The OFFICIAL studies it.)

    According to this you're twenty-eight.

MANN: Aye. It's a hard life.

    (The line begins to laugh, growing interested, behind
    him.)

OFFICIAL: Oh. A joker. *(He blows a whistle, hanging from*

74

a lanyard round his neck.) We'll see about that.

MANN: Don't bother. I'm just ... looking.

    (Two dock POLICE arrive; big.)

OFFICIAL: Troublemaker. Move him.

    (They step forward. MANN turns, crouches, arms
    curved downwards, like an orang-utan, the grip poised
    for swinging use.)

MANN: Easy now. I can find the way on my own.

OFFICIAL: *(Finally)* Let him be.

    (POLICE draw off. MANN turns to the table.)

MANN: Let's hope your line can show as much good sense.
    (He smiles gently.) The ticket.
    (The OFFICIAL hands it over, reluctantly and without
    grace.)

OFFICIAL: Don't try anything here again, I'm telling you.
    We've got ways of dealing with troublemakers.

MANN: *(Gently)* Good. You're going to need them.
    (Turning, a few paces towards the entrance.) If you
    bump into Mr Cuthbert Laws today, tell him you
    showed Tom Mann the door. He might strike you a
    special medal.

    (MANN walks off through the waiting seamen.)

OFFICIAL: Who'd he say he was? Who was it he said?

SEAMAN: Tom Mann, he said.

OFFICIAL: And who's Tom Mann when he's at home?

SEAMAN: Nobody. When he's at home. But he ain't at
    home, is he. He's in Liverpool.

5. FILM. BY GRAIN DOCK

MANN strides slowly along, taking in everything. Titles
up.

6. FILM. CITY STREET. STILL EARLY

MANN stops by a news-vendor's stall, buys a Manchester Guardian, asks for something else, is offered a small pad, gestures bigger with an angler's stretch of the hands, finally receives a large street map of Liverpool, which he pays for and tucks into his grip.

7. EXT. FILM. EXCHANGE STATION HOTEL

MANN stops, walks in.

8. INT. HOTEL FOYER

Red plush, deep curtaining, the odd discreet frond. The NIGHT PORTER, a young man, dozes at the desk. MANN approaches, pings the bell.

PORTER: *(Startled)* Yes, sir.

MANN: Could you tell me, do you have a Mr Cuthbert Laws, Secretary and General Manager of the Shipping Federation, staying here?

PORTER: One moment, sir, I'll have a look. *(Rummages through book.)* Er ... yes, we do, sir. Room seven. Just along the corridor. I imagine he'll be sleeping just now, sir.

MANN: *(Consulting watch)* Yes. Would you mind telling him there's a Mr Tom Mann to see him?

PORTER: What, now?

MANN: Now.

PORTER: *(Slowly)* Is he ... expecting you?

MANN: Mmmmm. Yes. I think you could say that.

PORTER: *(Going finally)* All right. If he's expecting you.

(The PORTER leaves. MANN fiddles the map out of the grip, spreads it on the desk, begins to study it. The PORTER returns after a little while. He's not pleased.)

PORTER: *(Stiffly)* Mr Cuthbert Laws has no wish to speak
    with you, sir.
    *(MANN studies the map a moment longer, then folds it,
    packs it away.)*
MANN: Is that so? Didn't he like being wakened?
PORTER: No, he didn't, sir. Not at all.
MANN: Tell him, will you, later on, you know, tell him
    he may have no wish to, but in a day or two he will
    have no choice in the matter. Will you tell him that?
PORTER: As you wish, sir.
MANN: You know, you say 'sir' as if you enjoyed it.
    (MANN leaves briskly, grip swinging.)

9. EXT. FILM
*MANN passes the dock offices of the large shipping lines,
finally approaches the Maritime Hall, headquarters of the
National Union of Seamen and Firemen, the Ship Stewards'
Union, the National Union of Dockworkers and the Mersey
Carters. He stands looking at the crazy over-busy
facade for a moment, then walks in.*

10. INT. A LONG DARK CORRIDOR, DOORS ON EITHER SIDE, A
LONG STRAIGHT STAIRCASE DIRECTLY AHEAD
*MANN stands, sunlight behind him, sniffs, pokes a door
open to the right, looks, pulls it to, repeats the process
to the left. A youth (GROARK), sixteen, seventeen, small,
skinny, carries mop-bucket and mop down the stairway.
Stops about four up as he sees the stranger.*
GROARK: Was there something?
MANN: *(Seeing him)* Aye. I'm looking for Committee Room
    'A', son.
GROARK: Oh. *(Pause)* Well, it's up here. *(Stands moment
    longer, then begins to plod back up the stairs,*

bucket splashing freely. MANN follows.)

11. INT. COMMITTEE ROOM 'A'

*Large, roomy, four windows on two walls, one pair giving
out on to the verandah that dominates the front of the
building, the other providing a fair view of the docks.
Down the centre, a long shiny deal table, with a dozen or
so hardback upright chairs. At the top of the table, a
single captain's chair, with arms and a bit of class. A
door in one corner leads to a small office. GROARK
pushes the door open, lets MANN in.*

GROARK: And less of the 'son'. All right?

(MANN smiles, back to GROARK.)

MANN: Sorry.

GROARK: *(Sniffing)* S'all right. I do a man's work.

(MANN is by the window, surveying the docks.)

GROARK: Strike Committee, are you?

MANN: Ahunh.

GROARK: Thought so. North End, is it?

*(MANN puts his grip down on the captain's chair,
takes out the map, opens it, fiddles thumbtacks from
his top pocket, carefully pins the map to the table
in front of his chair.)*

GROARK: *(Uneasy)* Hey, that's er, that's er, the, that's
the chairman's place, that it.

MANN: *(Evenly)* Aye.

GROARK: Jesus Christ! *(Closing eyes, opening them.)*
Eh, you coulda said. Bloodyell. You're him, aren't
you?

MANN: *(Busy)* Him. Yes.

GROARK: *(Stepping forward, wiping hand on apron)* I'm ...
I'm very pleased to make your acquaintance, brother.
I am that.

MANN: *(Taking his hand)* Greetings. Comrade.

GROARK: *(Stunned by the word, hand back too sharply)* Aye.
Aye. *(Lost now.)* Gerard Groark. That's me, that's
my name.

MANN: Good. Do you work here?

GROARK: Yes. I'm the er, I'm a steward. Waiting to go
on the boats.

MANN: *(Surveying room)* Fine. I'd like some breakfast,
Gerard. That all right?

GROARK: It is that, Mr ... brother. Egg and bacon do
you?

MANN: Eggs.

GROARK: Eh?

MANN: Eggs and bacon.

GROARK: Oh. Eggs and bacon. I have it. No more than a
jiff. *(He moves towards the door; turns, very
formal.)* I think I should like to say, on behalf of
the Maritime Hall management committee, how ...
honoured and ... privileged we are ... to have you
with us here ... in Liverpool. *(Pause)* I don't
think I step out of line by extending that ...
greeting to you on behalf of ... my colleagues.

MANN: Thank you, Brother Groark. It's an honour and a
privilege to be here. *(He takes out his big watch,
clicks it open.)* Could you get a word through to
Brother Frank Pearce? Tell him I've come.
*(GROARK stands staring, still realising it all, then
nods and leaves.)*

12. INT. MARITIME HALL. CORRIDOR AND STAIRWAY
*We see it from halfway up the stairs. It's crowded with
men spilling out from the bar parlour on the right,
jugs of porter in their fists. A door on the left opens,*

two men (GROARK and FRANK PEARCE) appear carrying a large
wooden filing cabinet. They shunt and buffet drinking
men in their way, as they approach the stairs.
PEARCE: (Thirty-five, dark, swarthy, short) Shift your
    bloody carcases, will you. I'm not taking this
    thing over youse.
    (Some groans and oaths.)
    (Last, GROARK already on the stairs) Now take your
    time lad, now take your time. We're not bloody
    mountain goats, you know. Leastways, I'm bloody not.
    Just nice and steady and we'll get the blinding
    thing up in one piece.
    (They begin the arduous ascent.)
    Now steady. Steady does it. STEADY FOR CHRIST'S
    SAKE. (They stop, disaster thinly avoided.) Christ
    almighty, what are you doing? (Props cupboard with
    knee, mops face with scarf.) I swear, it's a bloody
    madman we've gorrup there. We're supposed to be
    going on strike and I've never worked so bloody hard
    in me life. Right, come on. Let's get his blinding
    cabinet up while I've strength left.
    (They lumber on, PEARCE spattering the stairs with
    oaths and admonitions.)

13. COMMITTEE ROOM 'A'

The whole of the Strike Committee as at present
constituted - six men, counting PEARCE - is assembled.
It's noon or just after. The room is already dense with
smoke and heavy with noise. MANN is pouring himself a
glass of water at a table by a wall. He brings it back
to his chair, sits down. He sits, sipping his drink,
until the heated chat cools: the chair is deferred to.
MANN: (Looking around) Well.

*(Slow slide around the table: as we frame each
member of the Strike Committee, he makes his response.)*
JAMES SEXTON: All right. If we're ready. We'll
certainly take it back to the dockers.
THOMAS DITCHFIELD: We'll leave it to the seamen.
BILLAL QUILLIAM: The carters are ready for a signal.
Have been for a week or more.
*(The door opens and PEARCE and GROARK appear with the
cabinet.)*
PEARCE: Easy, lad, easy. Right, now back towards that
wall, *that* wall ... right, right, down gently,
gently, there she is. *(He stands, mops forehead with
neckerchief, sniffs.)* One filing cabinet. Liverpool
Strike Committee 1911 for the use of. *(To GROARK,
handing him a halfpenny.)* All right, go and get
yourself a mineral water.
(GROARK grins and leaves.)
MANN: Thank you, Frank.
*(PEARCE takes his seat at the bottom of the table,
picks up pen, inspects the open ledger book in
front of him.)*
PEARCE: Where are we then?
MANN: Still on timing, Frank. Dockers and carters
generally in favour.
PEARCE: *(Writing something)* All right. *(Finishing)* If
I can speak for the ship stewards for a moment, we're
already on record. We can go anytime. From now.
(Pause) Same goes for cooks.
*(MANN nods, begins the ascent of the table up the
other side.)*
MANN: What about the seamen and firemen, Terence?
TERENCE DIXON: Our call's been out for a week. We'll
go tomorrow, if that's the time to go.

MANN: *(Finally)* Good. Thank you brothers. *(He gets up,*
walks over to the filing cabinet, pulls a couple of
drawers open, looks inside, pushes them to again,
turns.) I shall want some files to go in there, Frank.
Tomorrow'll do. First thing. *(To whole Committee.)*
I'm not a great one for the past. It's what we do
now that counts. But there's one or two lessons to
be learnt. *(Pause)* I was involved in the big one,
'89, some of you will remember. I remember this. In
negotiation with the employers, time and time again
there'd be a point at issue - a particular rating,
the status of a special process - and the employer
would go straight to it, he'd have his documents
neatly pigeon-holed for reference. And us? Ours'd
be all over the floor, half a ton of it perhaps. It
finished up we had half a dozen men permanently on
their knees trying to sort it all out. *(Pause)* I want
to *win*, brothers. And I think we can. But it'll
only happen if we *organise*. And that means - *(He*
points to the cabinet) a system. I want that
filling. With information. I want copies of all
agreements for the past five years between employers
and the unions involved. I want detailed day-by-day
accounts of all negotiations undertaken by and on
behalf of this Joint Strike Committee. I want duty
rosters on file, so that *responsibility* can be
accurately assessed when things fall down. And I
want background on all the major shipping lines
involved in the Port of Liverpool. *(Grinning)* All
yours, Frank.

PEARCE: Eh, now wait a minute, I'm a full-time officer
of a union, brother, I can't be ...

MANN: We'll get you some help. It must be done.

82

(On quickly, moving back to the table, remaining standing.) Look, we are about to declare *war*. It's not summer manoeuvres we're about, brothers. It's war. Now then, this Strike Committee had better begin to get a few things straight. First, this Committee is the workers' general staff. Second, the job of a general staff is to deliver a victory by whatever means it has at its disposal. Third, I see myself as CGS, and it would help if you saw it that way too. *(He sits down.)* Questions.

DIXON: You'll have to find someat different to say to my seamen when you put it to 'em. They didn't elect *you* and you're not responsible to them.

(Some nods, grumbles of assent.)

MANN: All right, Terence. I'll find ... different words. I'm trying to make an important point about unity. Unity of purpose; unity of planning; unity of action. That's why I'm Secretary of the Transport Workers' Federation. That's why, isn't it, your union affiliated. All my life I've watched the single union fight its solitary battle against the full weight of employers and state. All my life, I've watched 'em getting hammered for want of support and solidarity from brother unions. *(Pause)* There are, need I remind you, brothers, eleven hundred and sixty-eight trade unions in this country. I reckon we need no more than fourteen. *(Pause)* I'm not up here to run a tea-party. Either we're fighting an all-out war or I'm off to Lime Street for the next train back.

(Silence. A few coughs.)

PEARCE: *(Finally)* I could put: 'Brother Mann's opening address on strategy was greeted with approving silence'.

the Shipping Federation. Five, the abolition of the engagement of seamen in the Shipping Federation offices. Six, the right of seamen to a portion of their wages in port during a voyage. Seven, the right of seamen to have a union representative present when signing on. Eight, hours of labour and rates and overtime to be fixed. Nine, improved forecastle accommodation.

MANN: The minimum rate, Brother Dixon. What are you asking?

DIXON: Six pounds and five pounds ten a month on mail steamers; five pounds ten and five pounds on ordinary cargo.

MANN: That's an increase of what?

DIXON: Ten bob a month on the best rates paid at present; about a pound on the worst.

MANN: Good. Thanks, Brother Dixon. *(Dixon sits.)* Frank?

PEARCE: *(Standing)* The stewards are demanding a minimum wage of four pounds a month, that's an increase of around thirty bob for most grades. We're asking for perquisites to be excluded from the reckoning. Galley staff are asking the same four pounds, plus four and six a day for work done in port. We're demanding the abolition of deductions to cover silver loss on voyage and we're asking for improved accommodation, like the seamen. We've had enough of the bloody 'glory hole'.

MANN: Thank you, Frank. *(Blowing cheeks.)* Right, answer me this then. How many men can we *count* on? I mean *really* count on? Brother Dixon?

DIXON: All of 'em. Twelve thousand.

PEARCE: And I've another ten and they're keen as pigeons to be off.

86

MANN: So where do we start?

DIXON: The Federation. If we crack them, we crack the
    lot. If they hold out, we sink.

MANN: Go on.

DIXON: The Shipping Federation controls sixty per cent
    of all shipping in this port. What they say goes.
    And they're the buggers who won't even *meet* the
    unions, let alone let us speak for the men. It's got
    to be them.

MANN: Frank?

PEARCE: S'right. Federation's the master.

MANN: But they control mainly cargo, isn't that right?

DIXON: That's right. About eighty per cent.

MANN: And the passenger boats are controlled by the big
    independent lines?

DIXON: That's right.

MANN: How many passenger boats are waiting crewing in
    port just now?

DIXON: Three.

MANN: What are they?

DIXON: Well, there's the *Baltic*, that's White Star.
    Then there's the *Teutonic*, she's White Star too. And
    erm ... *Empress of Ireland*. Canadian Pacific.

MANN: Sort of average is it, three a week, say?

PEARCE: Summer, yes. There's another four due the end
    of the week. Two for America, bringing back the
    swells for the Coronation.

MANN: Tut tut. What a pity. I suppose we could be
    arraigned for treason or something if *they* didn't
    get away.

DIXON: I'm not sure what you're driving at, brother.

MANN: *(Quietly)* I'm trying to see whether there isn't a
    better way of cracking the Federation than by hitting

87

it square on. You're closer to the ground than I am, but it occurs to me that we might be better off initially striking at the independents. Cargo's a funny thing. You don't fetch it this month, you fetch it next. You can't take it now, you take it when you can. Passengers're another story. They won't wait. If they can't go, they don't go. And that's a loss to the company that's irrecoverable.

PEARCE: So we put pressure on the independents through passengers. That makes some sense, I suppose. What then?

MANN: Well, we'll have to see. If things go well, we'll have the advantage of a sort of tide of successes to approach the Federation on. And there's nothing like success to bind a workforce together.

SEXTON: So where do *we* come in?

MANN: Dockers and carters carry on, at least for the time being. *(Grinning)* But it wouldn't do any harm to do a bit of ... what do they call it? - contingency planning for a week or two ahead.

DITCHFIELD: That's all right by us. Just so long as we know what's happening.

MANN: *(Tough)* You'll know what's happening, Brother Ditchfield, because this Committee will be meeting every day of the strike until we've brought it safely home. And you'll be here, helping to decide its policy. *(Looking at watch.)* I think we might break for a bite of someat now, Brother Secretary *(PEARCE nods assent.)*, before we launch into detailed strategies. *(Chairs screak back.)* *Before* you go, could I just outline what I think it's going to be useful to talk about for the rest of this particular meeting? *(Silence resumes.)* Perhaps you'd take some of this

down, Frank. It might serve as a sort of rough
agenda, bearing in mind that other members might wish
to table quite other matters. *(Pause)* We've to
discuss pickets. Nature, number, *style* of same.
We've to discuss co-ordination of all our activities
through and by this Joint Committee. We've to
discuss communications, both with the press and,
more important, the workers. To tell truth, I
couldn't give a cuss what the great, brutal British
public thinks, as long as the people I lead *know*
what's going on, understand it, agree with it, and
are prepared to abide by it. Strikes aren't won by
public sympathy: they're won by ruthless organisation,
concerted action, and understanding between leaders
and led. So: We shall need to discuss news-sheets,
demonstrations, speeches and the like. *(Pause)* We
shall need to discuss our relations with the police
and, if and when the time comes, with the army too.
It's idle to think that the Federation and the
Independents won't try to mobilise blackleg labour
from somewhere or other. So we've got to be on our
guard from the outset, if we want to avoid bloody
clashes between the picket lines and the law. Let's
get one thing clear: I'm not against violence. I
am against unarmed workers fighting street battles
against superior forces, be they police or the army.
(Pause) Well, that's some of the things I think we
should be talking about. Oh, two things before you
go off. I think we should have a leaflet run off
right away - perhaps you could put this in hand,
Brothers Dixon and Connor - letting the seamen know
it's tomorrow. And, I think it would be nice if we
could let everybody know we were in business. Be nice

if we let off a few rockets, the minute the strike's
declared. Sort of ... symbolic. *(He smiles sweetly.
The men return the smile, begin to leave.)*
PEARCE: *(Consulting watch)* Back at three, brothers, if
you will.
(They file out. PEARCE remains.)
You're riding them hard, brother.
MANN: *(Slowly)* It's ... a hard life, Frank.
*(PEARCE smiles, closes book, leaves. MANN gets up,
stretches, walks to the window overlooking the docks,
looks out. After a moment, a knock at the door, and
GROARK enters.)*
GROARK: What about some grub, brother?
MANN: *(Turning)* Mmmm. Good. Anything'll do. *(Pause)*
Oh. Do something for me, will you? Find a mattress
and a blanket from somewhere and put 'em in there.
(Gestures towards small office door.) Here's as good
a place as any, I reckon. *(Grinning)* I like to live
... close to my work.
GROARK: *(Smiling)* Right you are, Brother Mann. I'll do
that. Right after grub.
*(GROARK leaves. MANN returns to the table, begins to
trace routes through the docks on the map.)*

14. FILM. EXT. NIGHT. THE DOCKS
*Gaunt ships against the sky. Suddenly, a sheaf of rockets
rakes the skyline, and another, and still more.*

15. INT. OFFICE. NIGHT (5 A.M.)
*MANN under a blanket, stretched out on his mattress, a
lamp by his head, reading. The book is by Carlyle. He
studies it closely. His voice over, as he reads.*
MANN's VOICE: 'There is not a horse in England willing

90

and able to work but has due food and lodgings ...
And you say it is impossible. Brothers, I answer,
if for you it be impossible, what is to become of you?
It is impossible for us to believe it to be impossible.
The human brain, looking at these sleek English
horses, refuses to believe in such impossibilities
for Englishmen.' *(He stops reading, touches his nose
with his finger, returns to it again, says out loud:)*
'The human brain ... refuses to believe in such
impossibilities for Englishmen.' *(Pause)* I like
that. *(Pause)* I do.
*(Pan to floor by side of mattress. On it, the 'Red
Handbill':* It May Be Tomorrow.*)*

16. SLOW, EARLY MORNING SHOTS OF WATERFRONT
The three passenger steamships, Baltic, Teutonic *and*
Empress of Ireland *lie in dock. A picket of four men,
equipped with armbands, guards a gangway, well wrapped
against early-morning chills. A small boy approaches,
two brewcans in his hands. They tousle his hair, pour
tea and drink it, handing the lids round.*

Mix to:

17. MARITIME HALL.   EXT.   VERY QUIET

18.   INT.   COMMITTEE ROOM
*A woman (MARTHA CLARKE), thirty maybe, sits typing on
a table by a wall and window. There's a heap of files
by her chair, papers on both sides of her table. She is
neat, attractive, mature-looking. She wears her hair
pinned close to the head; long sleeved, high necked
brocade blouse and full ankle-length, very straight skirt.
She is absorbed in her work. MANN comes in from the*

'office' room, fiddling his jacket on over broad shoulders.
He stops when he sees the woman.

MANN: Good morning.

MARTHA: *(Finishing line, answering through it, then*
    turning) Morning.

MANN: *(Studying watch)* Will you be ... working here?

MARTHA: Mr Pearce set me on.

MANN: *(Yawning)* Ah. *(Still at watch.)* Still, it's early.

MARTHA: Seven-thirty. Mr Pearce said there was plenty
    to do. *(She gestures at the files on the floor.)*

MANN: I take it you're ... union.

    (MARTHA opens her handbag, takes out a small card,
    hands it to MANN. He looks at it, smiles, hands it
    back.)

    Good lass. *(Pause)* Sorry.

MARTHA: That's all right. You're right to ask.

    (MARTHA turns back to her work. MANN strides to the
    door, calls into the passageway.)

MANN: Gerry!

GROARK: *(OOV)* Yeah!

MANN: Eggs.

GROARK: On the way.

    (MANN closes the door, crosses to the table, sits
    down, begins to study some papers. MARTHA strips a
    page from the machine, clips it to some others on the
    desk, types a file heading on a strip of paper, licks
    and sticks it on to a file, puts the papers inside
    and carries it to the cabinet. She bends to place
    it into the bottom drawer. MANN watches her.)

MANN: I'm sorry, I haven't introduced myself. By name's
    Mann. Tom.

MARTHA: *(Standing)* Yes, I know. *(Pause)* I've seen your
    picture in the papers.

MANN: *(Grinning)* Don't flatter me, do they. Mek me look like an old walrus, stead of what I am ... deeply handsome.

(MARTHA laughs.)

Oh!

MARTHA: I didn't mean that. It just sounded so funny.

MANN: What's your name then?

MARTHA: Martha Clarke.

MANN: *(Standing, hand out)* I'm pleased to meet you, Martha.

(MANN and MARTHA shake hands, rather solemnly, then break and stand looking at each other. GROARK enters the room with a tray.)

GROARK: Morning. Eggs and papers.

MANN: Morning, Gerry. Put 'em on the table, will you.

(MARTHA returns to her seat rather quickly, resumes work. GROARK makes a great play of laying the breakfast out.)

MANN: *(Standing behind him)* Come on, Gerry, bloody hell, you're not on the boats yet, you know.

GROARK: *(Refusing to be hurried)* Got to get my hand in though. *(Standing back, surveying.)* Mmm. That looks all right. *(Moving to the door.)* Oh, there's a picture of you in the *Manchester Guardian*. *(Grin)* Can't say it does much for you. *(Pause)* Still, there isn't really that much to work on, is there?

(MANN makes a mock-menacing move towards the door; GROARK exits fast. MANN sits at table, begins to eat, spreads the Times, Manchester Guardian *and the* Mail *out around him, begins to read. We catch a* Guardian *headline: 'Seamen's Strike: a beginning made at several ports: Liverpool firms' offer'. There's a knock at the door and PEARCE and DIXON enter.)*

PEARCE: Morning, Tom. *(To MARTHA.)* Ah, you've arrived.
    Hello, Martha. *(He crosses to MARTHA, begins to
    discuss the work with her.)*

DIXON: *(Coldly)* Good morning.

MANN: *(Finishing breakfast)* Morning, brother.
    *(DIXON stands for a moment, then takes a seat at the
    table.)*
    (Finally) What's going on then?

DIXON: *(Taking note from pocket)* I'm not having this.
    (He throws the note on to the table.)

MANN: *(Taking note)* Oh. Why not?

DIXON: I take orders from Wilson in London. Nobody else.

MANN: *(Looking at note again)* I can't see any orders.

DIXON: I'm not having it. I'm not being told how to run
    my strike.

PEARCE: *(Returning)* Easy, Terence, easy now. There's no
    need to go ...

DIXON: Bugger easy. Either I run my bloody union or I
    don't. It's as simple as that. That note says I
    don't.

MANN: *(Reading)* 'Advise you reach no accommodation with
    leading independents until line has been agreed by
    Joint Committee. Signed Tom Mann, President,
    Joint Strike Committee.' I don't see how that stops
    you running your union, Brother Dixon.

DIXON: Look, I'm telling ...

MANN: *(Hard)* No, *you* look. You took a unilateral
    decision to meet with representatives of three major
    lines last night. The first we knew about it was
    when a *Manchester Guardian* reporter let it slip
    after the public meeting at the docks. Now, this is
    a *joint* Committee. If we're going to get anywhere,
    we're going to have to work *together*. I sent that

94

note with the full approval of the Committee - your
brothers, Brother Dixon - because I didn't want you
to reach any agreements that might weaken our
overall position. *(Pause)* I'm sorry if the tone
offended you. I am. Really.
(DIXON looks slightly mollified.)
But I had to put the Committee's position to you and
fast. Hence the note.

DIXON: I had the full backing of my executive for the
meeting with the companies.

MANN: I'm sure you did. But somebody's going to have to
tell your executive you're not in this on your own.
You won't take the knocks on your own; and you won't
take the perks either. *(Pause)* Perhaps I ought to have
a word with 'em.

PEARCE: *(Quickly)* I reckon that's Brother Dixon's job,
Tom.

MANN: Aye. Happen.
*(The situation appears defused. MANN gets up,
strides to door, opens it, steps into passage.)*
Gerry!

GROARK: *(OOV)* Yeah!

MANN: Coffee!

GROARK: *(OOV)* Right.

MANN: Four cups! *(He closes the door, returns to the
table.)* So what happened?

DIXON: We met Cunards, Holts and White Star.

MANN: What level?

DIXON: General Managers.
(MANN pulls a wondering face.)

MANN: And?

DIXON: *(Smugly)* They've conceded pretty well everything.

MANN: Oh?

DIXON: It's true. Full agreement on eight of the nine
    demands. If we can carry on like this, we'll be
    home and dry within a week.

MANN: Ahunh. And the stewards?

DIXON: *(Looking at PEARCE)* Stewards weren't present.
    I imagined they'd be meeting ... later on.

PEARCE: No. We ... didn't meet. We brought it back
    to the Joint Committee.

    (Long silence. Some discomfort, for DIXON.)

DIXON: We'll not settle without the stewards. There's
    no question of that.

    (Another silence.)

MANN: When you say 'full agreement', are you talking
    about ... particular ships, or about all ships of the
    three lines you mentioned?

DIXON: Well, we were talking initially about particular
    ships ...

MANN: The *Baltic*, the *Teutonic*, so on.

DIXON: But I see no reason why ...

MANN: But as yet you have agreement only on the basis
    of half a dozen *ships*. *(Pause)* Is that right?

DIXON: That's right.

    (Pause)

MANN: *Did* you sign anything?

DIXON: *(Defiantly)* No.

MANN: And when do you meet again?

DIXON: Today.

MANN: Where?

DIXON: Exchange Station Hotel.

MANN: Make it ... here.

DIXON: Why?

MANN: You've met there once already. They should meet
    on your ground now. And I want to be present. In a

leading role.

DIXON: *(Finally)* They won't come.

    (GROARK in with coffee.)

MANN: Ah, thanks, Gerry. *(Pause, watching.)* And one for
    Martha over there. *(MARTHA smiles to have it.)*
    Grand. Many thanks.
    (GROARK out.)
    They'll come.

19. EXT. FILM. MARITIME HALL APPROACH AND EXTERIORS

*Three automobiles neatly parked in line. The drivers
lean on wings, in a knot, chatting.*

20. INT. COMMITTEE ROOM

*MANN in chair. DIXON on his right hand. PEARCE on left.
MARTHA with notepad, facing MANN. The three company men
down table sides. They are: MONTAGUE (Cunard);
CARRINGTON (Holt); MENTEITH (White Star).*

MANN: Well, there are actually several reasons why your
    boats might not get away on the evening tide,
    Mr Menteith. In the first place, you have made no
    agreement with the stewards' union. In the second,
    we are simply not interested in agreements that
    cover individual ships. Let me quote from this
    morning's *Manchester Guardian*, gentlemen, though I'm
    sure I've no need to. Mr Cuthbert Laws, General
    Manager of the Shipping Federation, is reported as
    saying, I quote: 'Even if the men win better wages
    now, it will not do them much good. We shall be
    here day after day, every time a crew signs on,
    whittling away the increase until it disappears.
    We are always here. The men's union is here only
    once and again.' *(He looks benignly up, smiles.)*

Mmm. We want that changing. The agreement we put our
names to will cover every ship in your line. In
return, every ship in your line will be immediately
placed on the white list of every port in the country.
(Pause) Those are our conditions, gentlemen.
(Standing abruptly.) I think we can leave the
detailed negotiations in the hands of brother Dixon
and your good selves.
*(The three company men stand, not at all sure of
their ground.)*

MENTEITH: You realise we'll need full board approval for
agreement covering the whole company.

CARRINGTON: That's right.

MANN: Yes I do. *(Pause)* May I suggest the telegraph
service. It has many advantages. Especially as time
and tide wait for no man.

MENTEITH: We'll see what can be done.

MANN: Thank you for coming, gentlemen. Your good sense
is an example to the whole shipowning fraternity. I've
little doubt it will be seen as such.
*(The three company men leave, stiff bows but no
handshakes.)*
(Grinning) We're on the way, brother.
(DIXON grins back.)

21. EXT. (BUT COULD BE STUDIO)   THE UPSTAIRS VERANDAH
AT THE MARITIME HALL

Immediately outside the committee room windows, on the wall,
INTERNATIONAL SEAFARERS' CLUB AND INSTITUTE: SEAMEN'S
UNION: FEDERATED WITH ALL THE SEAMEN'S UNIONS OF THE
WORLD. And below: MARITIME HALL. Sounds of large crowd
gathered. Some banners obtrude; one in particular:
'War is now declared. Strike home and strike hard for

liberty' (there is a very good picture of this, that can be
worked while MANN's speech is in progress). MANN, CU,
addresses the crowd.

MANN: Brothers. *(Noises down.)* Brothers, we have come a
long way. In twelve days we've won massive
concessions from more than sixty-five per cent of
owners: the full ten shillings a month for seamen
and firemen, full union recognition, an agreed
minimum wage, vastly improved conditions and
accommodation, and much, much more. For the stewards,
well, we fell five shillings short of the four pounds
a month we laid claim to, but we've improved on
everything else: shore duty pay, conditions and
accommodation, overtime pay. *(Pause)* We're doing well,
brothers. *(Loud and prolonged cheering.)* But we've
some way to go before we reach port. Having so far
won the strike and gained all these benefits from
the biggest shipping firms of the country, we must
now extend our operations to the remaining lines, most
of which are controlled by the bitterest enemies of
the workers - the Shipping Federation. These firms
have absolutely refused - and refuse still - to
consider our demands or recognise the unions. *(Pause)*
The District Joint Strike Committee have therefore
decided to withdraw all union sailors and firemen and
cooks and stewards from the boats of the Federation
firms, beginning Monday morning, June 26th. *(Great
cheering.)* Any men continuing to work on these
vessels will be considered and dealt with as
blacklegs. They will be no different - and will
receive no different treatment - from those ...
things that crawl off the Federation's depot ships
anchored off Prince's Dock, collected, one imagines,

in jamjars, like maggots, from every upturned stone in Britain, and brought to Liverpool in a feeble, festering attempt to break the strike. *(Pause)* I must say, while I'm on the subject, how responsibly the pickets continue to handle this ... difficult situation. Let it remain so. *(Sombre)* Few of you will need reminding that a picket was shot through the head in Hull two days ago, and died later in hospital. *(Pause. With grim emphasis.)* It must not happen here. If the flow of blackleg labour continues, now, the shipowner will be forced to rely upon our fellow unionists the carter, the docker, the coalie, the craneman, the scaler, the railwayman and the engineer to wage war against his brothers now on strike, in loading, discharging, and working at his blackleg vessels. *(Pause)* Our fellow transport workers in Glasgow, Goole, Hull and Southampton have refused to be the catspaws of the shipowner, and all eyes are now turned upon Liverpool men, anxiously watching whether they will exhibit solidarity, or whether the evils of sectionalism shall curse our movement once more and seal the fate of the seafaring man for years to come. The Strike Committee are confident that no such calamity shall happen, and that our brothers, now that they are appealed to, will immediately put their already expressed sympathy into direct action, and refuse to be guilty of handling any goods or in any way assisting the vessels of Federation lines. *(Pause)* The strike begins first thing on Monday morning. Strike at once, strike hard, and as men be men!

(Sustained cheering. MANN waves, steps off balcony into committee room, followed by rest of Strike

Committee.   The cheering continues.)
Right. I think we might be hearing from Mr Cuthbert
Laws before long.
DITCHFIELD: We'll have to get busy. I've to get
this through eighteen carters' branches before I can
call 'em out.
SEXTON: I've twenty-two. At four meetings a day, that's
nearly a week.
MANN: I've a feeling we shan't need you. Neither
dockers nor carters. I've a feeling we've won
already, brothers. There's a strong wind blowing
up around Mr Laws's house of cards.

22.   EXCHANGE STATION HOTEL.   VESTIBULE

MANN sits in a plush armchair, under a huge rubber tree.
He's asleep, head forward. A PORTER approaches.
PORTER: Mr Mann. *(Nothing)* Mr Mann. *(Nothing. He leans*
forward and pokes MANN's shoulder with his finger.)
Mr Ma ... *(MANN has his finger inside his fist. They*
look at each other for a moment.) Mr ... Laws will
see you now, sir.
(MANN sniffs, slowly releases the finger, gets up.
The PORTER turns and leads him off down a heavily
carpeted corridor.)

23.   LAWS'S ROOM

LAWS, in dressing gown, drinks a brandy, smokes a corona.
The remains of a room dinner rest on a tray on the table.
It's a big, comfortable, tasteful room, a little heavy,
perhaps, in its furnishings.   LAWS is youngish; late
thirties say.   Haut-bourgeois, bland, cool, able.   He
has some wit but no humour.
Knock at door.

LAWS: Come.

    (The PORTER enters.)

PORTER: Mr Mann, sir.

    (The PORTER stands aside as MANN enters.)

LAWS: Ah, Mr Mann, how nice to see you. *(To PORTER.)*
    Thank you, that will be all. *(Looking around.)*
    Well, then, won't you have a seat. Can I get you a
    drink?

MANN: *(Sitting down)* No, thanks.

LAWS: *(Catching something in the tone)* Oh. Don't you
    approve?

MANN: I don't mind if you drink. I don't ... approve of
    it for myself.

    (LAWS smiles, raises his glass in an ironic salute,
    drains it, pours another.)

LAWS: Good of you to come so soon. *(MANN impassive.)*
    We've ... we've studied your demands. And ... we
    don't think a great deal of them. *(Pause)* I thought I
    should let you know, there's a strong move afoot to
    start laying up.

    (Silence)

    I take it you know what that could mean for the men.
    Let alone the country.

MANN: Let alone the employers.

    (Silence)

LAWS: Yes. *(Pause)* Fortunately, I think we've managed
    to stave off that particular ... extreme line of
    action.

MANN: Glad to hear it.

LAWS: *(Very straight)* The Federation is not in a position
    at this moment in time to grant recognition to the
    unions. We cannot accept the total defeat that
    that would imply. If you ... persist in demanding it,

I think several of the lines would almost certainly lay up their ships and wait until the clouds cleared. However long that took. *(Pause)* Do you take my meaning?

MANN: You have, I take it, a compromise to offer.

LAWS: Yes. *(Pause. Gathering.)* I've suggested that each company within the Federation enters into individual negotiation with the appropriate unions. That way, the issue can be speedily resolved without compromising the Federation's stance. *(Pause)* How does that strike you?

MANN: *(Slowly)* I think we'd probably view that very favourably. Pragmatically, we achieve our ends. I don't think we're bothered about the protocols. *(Pause)* I'll take it back.

LAWS: It's not just seamen, firemen and stewards. You'd have to call off the threatened strike of all port workers - dockers, carters, coalheavers, railmen, all of them. While the negotiations are in progress, I mean.

MANN: The Strike Committee controls the port, Mr Laws. If we say work, there is work.

LAWS: *(Smiling bleakly)* That must give you ... immense satisfaction, Mr Mann.

MANN: Objectively, yes. Personally, none at all. I'd sooner be working a farm. Growing things. *(He stands up abruptly.)* I should be able to let you know by tomorrow.

LAWS: I look forward to a favourable reply.
(Their hands waver, as though a handshake is called for, but nothing happens. MANN makes for the door.)
My father used to tell me about you. He fought you in '89. Perhaps you remember.

MANN: Yes. I remember.

LAWS: Why do you do it? Go on doing it, I mean.

MANN: *(Simply)* To rid the world of people like you, Mr Laws. *(He leaves.)*

24. HOTEL VESTIBULE

PEARCE paces anxiously up and down. MANN appears, sees him first.

MANN: Hello, Frank. Keeping in trim, are you?

PEARCE: Christ! Tom. Look, I don't know what you've been saying to Laws but we've got problems.

MANN: I don't doubt it. Talk.

PEARCE: *(Terse)* The dockers are out.

MANN: How do you mean? Called?

PEARCE: No. Just out.

MANN: How many?

PEARCE: Five thousand. Mebbe more. Half the blinding work force.

MANN: Sexton?

PEARCE: Down there. Working like a goblin.

MANN: And?

PEARCE: They don't like goblins.

MANN: Let's go.

(MANN and PEARCE leave quickly.)

25. ACTUALITY FILM

Food, fuel, etc., stands on trucks and carts. Knots of dockers stand idle. Nothing moves.

26. EXT. FILM

MANN and PEARCE on dockside. Speak to group of men, who point them in direction of large hut. They continue towards it.

27. INT. HUT

Meeting place of Dockers' Union No 12 Branch. Inside,
SEXTON, a gash in his head, being attended to by another
union official. The room is empty save for them. MANN
and PEARCE in.

MANN: What's it about, brother?

SEXTON: *(Savage)* It's a bloody insurrection, that's what
it's about. They're out, Tom.

MANN: I know they're out. What I want to know is why.

SEXTON: I told you. Don't say I didn't tell you.
Liverpool dockers ...

MANN: Shag Liverpool dockers! I'm not interested in
sodding *Liverpool* dockers, I'm interested in *workers*.
What's this *about*, brother. We've got the Federation
in the palm of our hand, all we need is two days more,
of discipline and unity and solidarity, and what do
we get!

SEXTON: *(Standing, groggy but angered)* Look, don't start
blaming me. If I'd spent more time with the men
instead of up there with your blasted Strike Committee,
perhaps this'd never've happened. Any of it.

MANN: *(Cooling)* All right. All right, Jim, I'm sorry.
How's the head?

SEXTON: All right. Bloody awful, actually. If I get hold
of the bastard who threw it, he'll learn a thing or
two.

MANN: You spoke.

SEXTON: Yeah. Mass meeting, north frontage. They
wouldn't listen. Strike, strike, they yelled. Strike,
strike. I put the Joint Committee line, they just
didn't want to know. There's a dozen branches gone
already, more to follow, I should think.

MANN: And what're they after? Do you know?

SEXTON: Aye. Union recognition. Twopence an hour. New overtime rates. And a fifty-four-hour week.

MANN: Christ almighty! They don't want a boat each for Christmas as well do they? *(Pause)* Who's in charge, Jim?

SEXTON: *(Offended)* I'm in charge!

MANN: Come *on*, James. You're sitting with a hole in your head.

SEXTON: *(Reluctant)* Word has it, Milligan, No 12 Branch.

MANN: Who's he then?

SEXTON: Nobody. Just a bloody straightforward foursquare up and down honest as the day is long firebrand.

28. INT. MARITIME HALL. STAIRWAY, EMPTY

A young man, MILLIGAN, steps in from the bright sunshine.
He's lean, hard, lithe, a little over average height;
wears a short, full-face beard and longish hair. He
stands in the hallway, adjusting to the shadows. GROARK
opens a door, enters the corridor.

MILLIGAN: *(Irish)* Committee Room 'A'.

GROARK: Upstairs, first right.

   (MILLIGAN hits the stairs hard, takes them two at a
   time, reaches the door, knocks once, opens on the
   knock.)

29. INT. COMMITTEE ROOM

MANN's at the filing cabinet. MARTHA CLARKE works at her
little table. MANN continues his search, though he's
aware of MILLIGAN's presence.

MILLIGAN: Milligan.

MANN: *(Turning finally)* Mann. Come in.

   (MILLIGAN shuts the door, looks round the room.)

MILLIGAN: You wanted words.

106

MANN: That's right. Sit down, won't you.

    (MILLIGAN sits reluctantly. MANN goes on with his search. MARTHA half turns, smiles at MILLIGAN; who half returns the smile, but not quite. MANN makes the table finally, dumps three files untidily down in front of him, sits down to face MILLIGAN. Stares at him for a long time.)

MANN: *(Slowly)* More than five thousand dockers out. In flat contravention of the union's declared policy of *selective* support for the seamen's claims. Sexton says it's you.

MILLIGAN: Sexton should know better.

MANN: How do you mean?

MILLIGAN: Can't be one man. However ... gifted.

    (Pause)

MANN: How do *you* see it?

MILLIGAN: I think we've gorra case.

MANN: I'm *sure* you've gorra case. *Now's* just not the time to be presenting it.

MILLIGAN: Who says so?

MANN: I say so. Your union says so. The Joint Committee says so.

MILLIGAN: The dockers say you're wrong.

MANN: *(Bleakly now)* Do they?

MILLIGAN: Ask 'em. They'll tell you.

    (Silence)

MANN: Martha, could you nip out for some sandwiches. Couple of big uns. *(To MILLIGAN.)* All right? Cheese and onion, love.

MARTHA: Do you want sauce?

MANN: *(Looking at MILLIGAN)* No. No sauce. *(He hands MARTHA a sixpence.)* And get something for yourself. *(MARTHA leaves. He closes the door after her, stands,*

leans with back against it. Finally:) You wouldn't be
working for them, would you?

MILLIGAN: You want a belt in the mouth, brother, you just
carry on like that.

MANN: *(Unperturbed)* I can't think of any other
explanation.

MILLIGAN: Look, I'm warning you, I don't care who you are
or how old you are, you go on ...

MANN: Can you? Eh? How else can you explain it? Eh?

MILLIGAN: ... with that rubbish and I'll put you down,
I'm war ...

MANN: You must be. A Laws man. You must be.

MILLIGAN: Right. I've told you.

*(MILLIGAN lunges, MANN catches him with a perfect
short uppercut to the stomach, takes him, with
immensely powerful arms, by the shoulders and bangs
him headfirst into the door; then throws him at the
table, where he lies spreadeagled across it, moaning
and clutching his stomach. His nose bleeds quite a
lot. MANN wipes his hands fastidiously on his
handkerchief, crosses to the table, takes MILLIGAN by
the lapels and helps him to a seat.)*

MANN: I'm sorry. I provoked that. I couldn't help
myself. I just needed ... that release. Are you
all right?

MILLIGAN: *(Struggling to breathe)* I've ... I've ... I've
known ... days I've ... felt better. Jesus Christ.

MANN: *(Dabbing MILLIGAN's nose)* Here. Let's clean you up.
*(MILLIGAN takes the handkerchief, dabs his nose and
mouth with it, lurches to his feet, does a few deep
squats, begins to breathe more steadily.)*

MILLIGAN: Christ. Someone shoulda told me about you.

MANN: I'm sorry. I really am.

MILLIGAN: Yeah. Yeah. It's all right.

MANN: *(Hand out)* All right?

MILLIGAN: *(Taking it, blowing)* All right.

MANN: I had to be sure.

MILLIGAN: Yeah.

(MANN and MILLIGAN sit down again.)

MANN: You've ... put us in a spot, brother. Now I want
   you to help us out of it. If the dockers stay out,
   the carters'll probably follow, and there'll be no
   settlement for the seamen with the cargo companies.
   That's to say, with the Federation.

MILLIGAN: I thought the Federation wouldn't play anyway.
   If the dockers don't strike, they'll go on using
   black labour till the seamen have all died in their
   boots.

MANN: No. We've got a deal. Supplies of blacklegs are
   running low. And the good weather's making most of
   the cargo particularly vulnerable to delay. They've
   offered to negotiate on an individual company basis.
   (Pause) We've as good as won.
   (Long pause.)

MILLIGAN: I see.

MANN: Now. What do we do?

MILLIGAN: I don't know. *(Pause)* These aren't wild men
   making wild demands, you know. These are people
   driven daft by overwork and underpay.

MANN: You don't have to tell me, son.

MILLIGAN: I can't see 'em going back without someat.

MANN: Go on.

MILLIGAN: Well, at the very least, total recognition of
   the union by the whole port authority. And clear and
   unequivocal union preference in hiring practice.

MANN: Mmm.

MILLIGAN: Even so, it's hard to say what they'll do.

MANN: Well. We'd better get started. *(Pause)* I'd ... er
... like you to join us.

MILLIGAN: Mmm?

MANN: Joint Strike Committee.

MILLIGAN: No, no. That's not me at all. Jesus Christ!

MANN: Mebbe not then. But it is now. I'll see that
appointment's ratified by this evening.

MILLIGAN: What about Sexton?

MANN: I think you should get started.

MILLIGAN: All right. Whatever you say.
(They shake hands, rather formally.)

MANN: Seven o'clock sharp. Here.
*(MILLIGAN nods, leaves. MANN paces the room, looks
out of the window, fretting. MARTHA comes in with the
sandwiches wrapped in thin muslin.)*

MARTHA: Two cheese and onion.

MANN: *(At table)* Thanks. *(Opening one.)* No sauce? *(MARTHA
goes to answer. MANN grins. She grins back.)*

MARTHA: I saw Milligan on the stair. He looks as if he'd
had a fall. His nose was a mess. *(MANN chews his
sandwich impassively.)* Oh. Gerry gave me this. *(She
hands MANN a note.)* A Federation messenger brought it
by hand. I said I'd bring it up.
(MANN rips it open. Reads it carefully; face tight.)
Bad news?

MANN: *(Stony)* Not good.

30. COMMITTEE ROOM

*Full Strike Committee meeting. Full of smoke. It's late
into the night. MARTHA takes notes. MILLIGAN, MANN,
DIXON and DITCHFIELD are in shirtsleeves. QUILLIAM
remains fully suited, as do SEXTON and PEARCE. It's a hot,*

sultry night. *From below, the noise of carousing seamen.*

SEXTON: Well, I don't think there's any doubt they'll stay out. How long is anyone's guess. But I've had reports from every branch during the day, and there's no sign of 'em budging, for the present.

MANN: Brother Milligan?

MILLIGAN: 'Fraid so. They're listening to nobody. And I think the picket clash with the police up the North End's just the first of many.

MANN: Ahunh. I think we can take it that the owners aren't bluffing either. *(Reading a note on the table before him.)* 'Failing a return to work by 6 a.m. Friday, the shipping dock employers will declare a lock-out of all dockers in the port.' I like the economy of style. Whatever else they waste, it's rarely words.

PEARCE: So. What do we do?

DIXON: We've got to get them back.

QUILLIAM: And how do you suggest we do it?

DIXON: *I* don't know. It's not *my* union.

SEXTON: I've called dockgate meetings for tomorrow. I suggest every Strike Committee member attend at least one. And I think we should start running off hand-bills and posters spelling out the Committee's case for discipline and unity.

MANN: I suppose that's a start. Anything else?

DITCHFIELD: I reckon we ought to do something about staunching my lot. They'll be next, I can feel it in me water.

QUILLIAM: Somebody ought to be talking to the employers. At least we ought to have a go at persuading them to postpone the lock-out, if only on the grounds that it'll lead inevitably towards worsening the overall

situation. *(He receives doleful looks all round.)*
All right.   It was only a suggestion.
(Silence.)

MILLIGAN: *(Putting it together carefully)* Quite frankly,
I don't think we've got a chance in five thousand of
getting the dockers back before the lock-out.
Whatever we do, things've gone too far now. So, in a
way, aren't we starting at the wrong end?

SEXTON: *(Hostile)* Meaning?

MILLIGAN: Meaning, wouldn't we be better backing the
dockers' claims than making fools of ourselves trying
to get them to do something they quite clearly aren't
going to do?
*(Momentary silence. Then a whole spate of rejections
from the members, especially SEXTON, DITCHFIELD and
PEARCE (all top union officials).)*

SEXTON: You can't ratify unofficial action just because
it has the upper hand, man. Surely you ...

DITCHFIELD: Bad practice. No union could hold its head
up after that, believe you me.

PEARCE: No. Let them come to us. That way there's
discipline. The other way there's only anarchy and
chaos.

MANN: *(Matter of fact)*   Much as I hate disagreeing with
old and trusted colleagues, I think he's right.

PEARCE: You what? You think he's what?

MANN: I think he's *right*. Sooner or later, we have got to
face the cruel but incontrovertible fact that we have
lost control. We can no longer, if you'll pardon the
expression, deliver the goods. Now, the longer we go
on trying to whip the dockers in, the more evident
that fact becomes. And all the time, of course, we
lose sight of the enemy who remains, need I remind you,

112

the capitalist employer. *(Pause. Some mutters.)* Let's, anyway, just for ... argument's sake, examine the case for an offensive. No, listen. *(They subside.)* Suppose we endorsed the dockers' claims – not all of 'em, but enough to carry them with us. Suppose, then, Brother Ditchfield, we invite the carters to join them. With one or two claims of their own, of course. Take it a step further. There are signs that the railwaymen in these parts are looking for an opportunity to kick over the 1907 Conciliation Boards and do some face-to-face bargaining. Now, imagine us taking the railwaymen with us. Mmm? And suppose, too, that the tramwaymen came out; and the sanitary men; and the scavengers; and the electricity plant workers; and the gas workers; and the bakers. Mmm? Where do you think we are *then*, brothers? Cap in hand? Or boot on the collar? *(He sits back, aglow with the prospect.)*

PEARCE: That's a mite fanciful, init Tom?

MANN: You say that line ... beautifully, Frank. Every time.

DIXON: Still, it's a far cry.

DITCHFIELD: Aye.

QUILLIAM: Is it feasible?

MANN: I shouldn't think so. *(Grinning hugely.)* Why don't we just *do* it. We could start by issuing a statement of unequivocal support for the dockers. How's this, Martha? Erm ... 'The Strike Committee are of the opinion that the dockers, who have rendered such effective service to the seamen and firemen, stewards and cooks, are acting quite within reason in asking that, in return, those unions should now assist them to obtain the recognition of their union, to which they attach so much importance and which, we agree, is

113

a matter of vital concern. Erm ... in only a few
instances will that involve any immediate increase of
pay, and even then it will only mean a return to the
conditions which formerly obtained.' How does that
sound?

PEARCE: *(Ironically)* Sounds grand, Tom. *Sounds* grand.
If I were to try to put my finger on a weakness in
your case - and God forbid it should fall to me to
have to do it - I think it would be round about where
you slip in ... the railwaymen. Now you see, without
them, I don't think your case is worth a bag of cold
peas. And I can't for the life of me see how you're
going to get them involved. Unless you've someat
up your sleeve. *(Grinning)* Always likely, of course.

MANN: Arms, Frank. Only arms. *(Pause)* Though, strangely
enough, I did take a quiet stroll yesterday around
St George's Square with the North-West Secretary of the
Amalgamated Society of Railway Servants, who is of the
opinion that, if their grievances are not met by the
end of the week, he can see no alternative but to put
the matter ... in the hands of this Committee.
(A long silence.)

(Very grave now.) I'm sorry to have been so light in
manner over this. It is, indeed, our most important
moment. Almost by accident we find ourselves on the
brink of a major offensive, in which the whole of
this city will be our battlefield, and where victories
and defeats will be of moment to others far and wide
throughout this land. It seeme to me that we have no
choice but to go on. But if we do go on, we must do
so with iron purpose and resolute intent. There is no
such manoeuvre as an apologetic attack. We must aim
to deliver a crushing defeat to the shipowning

fraternity, one that they will remember for years and years to come. *(Pause)* In the meantime, we must prepare ourselves for counter-offensives of much greater power and magnitude than any we have had to deal with before.
(We mix to actuality sequences (still or film) of the army arriving; foot soldiers and cavalry; rotting food on trucks; soldiers and police escorting food convoys through the streets of Liverpool; police on horseback pursuing demonstrating strikers; pickets clashing with police and army; gunboats in the Mersey; soldiers on the railways; armoured cars patrolling the streets; newspaper headlines detailing the state of civil strife that has developed; women and children proclaiming rent strikes; mass meetings of striking workers. A gradual build-up of sound is required too.) As we aim to control the day-to-day life of the city, so the state and the civic authorities will aim to wrest that control from us. We will be confronted not merely by staves and truncheons but by rifles and cold steel. Gunboats may well guard the depot ships and the docks. Every effort will be made to discredit our cause and undermine our morale. We will need the highest possible sort of self-discipline, if we are not to offer ourselves up to the slaughter. *(Back to MANN, now, BCU.)* And even then, we may not escape it.

34. EXT. FILM. EARLY MORNING. A BRIGHT SUMMER DAY
MANN and QUILLIAM walk around St George's Square and Plateau, deserted save for the pigeons and a few labourers erecting the speakers' platforms for the afternoon's rally and demonstration. MANN is reading something aloud, QUILLIAM listening intently.

MANN: 'Don't disgrace your parents, your class, by being
        the willing tool any longer of the Master Class. You,
        like us, are of the slave class. When we rise, you
        rise; when we fall, even by your bullets, ye fall
        also. You no doubt joined the army out of poverty.
        We work long hours for small wages at hard work,
        because of our poverty. And both your poverty and
        ours arises from the fact that Britain belongs to
        only a few people. Think things out and refuse any
        longer to murder your kindred. Help us to win back
        Britain for the British, and the World for the
        Workers.'

QUILLIAM: It's good.

MANN: I know it's good. Is it actionable?

QUILLIAM: *(Thinking)* I'm not rightly sure.

MANN: Well you're the lawyer, Billie.

QUILLIAM: Yes. It probably is.

MANN: Right. So do I say yes to printing it?

QUILLIAM: Well, if you mean are they likely to bring
        charges against the *publishers*, the answer's almost
        certainly no.

MANN: *(Sniffing)* Wouldn't matter anyway. It needs saying.
        Now more than ever. We'll publish.
        (MANN and QUILLIAM reach a platform.)
        How many do you reckon, s'afternoon.

QUILLIAM: A lot. Perhaps a hundred thousand counting the
        wives and kids. *(Pause)* It ... hardly seemed possible,
        only weeks ago.

MANN: What?

QUILLIAM: All this. Seamen, dockers, carters, coalies,
        cranemen, engineers, tramwaymen. And now five
        thousand railmen, and growing every day. Nothing
        moves, but we say it should.

116

MANN: *(Smiles)* It's ... as it should be, Billie. No
more than proper. *(Pause)* It'll be good today. It's
what we need. And it'll serve to demonstrate *(A squad
of horses clatters past)* to that lot, that we have
both spirit and discipline greatly in excess of their
own.

QUILLIAM: Let's hope so.

MANN: It will. It will.

*(A short wiry man walks towards them, a sort of
rough-hewn stave in his hands.)*

STRANGER: Are you brother Mann?

MANN: Aye. I hope that thing doesn't mean mischief.

STRANGER: So do I. I work for Terrell's, the sawyers by
Harvey Brew. We've had this order in for three
hundred staves. Like this one. I tried to find out
who for, but no one were saying. This morning, police
came round to fetch 'em. I thought you should know.
*(MANN takes the stave, weighs it in his hands, hands
it back to STRANGER.)*

MANN: Thank you, brother.

(MANN holds his hand out. The STRANGER takes it.)

STRANGER: You're welcome, brother. *(Pause)* See you on the
march.

(The STRANGER leaves. MANN looks at QUILLIAM.)

MANN: What do you think?

QUILLIAM: I think you'd better go and find out.

32. POLICE HEADQUARTERS. THE OFFICE OF THE CHIEF
SUPERINTENDENT

*The SUPERINTENDENT sits trimming his moustaches before a
mirror placed on his desk. He's a tall, florid, handsome
man, about forty-five; rather vain and showy. A knock at
door; a constable opens it, says 'A Mister', and MANN is in.*

117

MANN: Mann. Good morning, Superintendent.

SUPERINTENDENT: *(Only momentarily surprised)* Morning, Mr Mann. Nice to see you again. *(To door.)* All right. *(The constable leaves.)* Just let me finish this perishing thing, will you. Seems to grow faster in the heat. *(He tweeks away at it, rather lovingly.)* Can't think why. *(He finishes, regards himself affectionately in the mirror, sweeps his equipment into the drawer, the clippings into his hand and thence a basket, and turns to devote his whole attention to MANN, who is seated in a bucket chair opposite.)* Well, Mr Mann. To what do I owe the erm pleasure, as they say?

MANN: *(Quiet, contained)* Just a last minute precaution. I wanted to be quite sure we understood each other regarding this afternoon's proceedings.

SUPERINTENDENT: Why, of course we do, Mr Mann. We spoke only, what, two or three days ago. Is there something wrong?

MANN: I hope not, Superintendent. As I understand it, we have agreed to marshall the four marches and the assembly in the Plateau. You, in turn, have indicated a willingness to remain out of sight and unobtrusive as possible.

SUPERINTENDENT: That's right.

MANN: And you have seen and approved Mr Shelmerdine's permitting letter for the use of the Square and Plateau.

SUPERINTENDENT: What is all this about, Mr Mann?

MANN: *(Tersely)* Just this. A hundred thousand people - mostly men, but some women and children - will come to the centre of Liverpool this afternoon. You haven't agreed to let us 'police' them because you like

118

surrendering your power and authority; you've done
it because you know perfectly well that if you even
tried to do it you'd probably be trampled underfoot.
(Pause) There's a very thin line, Superintendent,
between order and chaos. You tread it this afternoon.
A foot wrong and the Mersey'll rise a foot more by
nightfall. With largely innocent blood. *(Pause)* Do
you take my meaning?

SUPERINTENDENT: Perfectly, Mr Mann. It's no more than
you said the other day. A bit more ... poetical,
perhaps, but basically the same message. One, as you
know, I've already taken delivery of.

MANN: I believe you took delivery of several hundred
specially prepared staves this morning.

SUPERINTENDENT: Did we? Is it ... to the point?

MANN: You know ... nothing about them?

SUPERINTENDENT: Nothing. They could be drill sticks, I
suppose. Now that we're working closely with the army,
we're having to improve our training procedure. Yes,
I think you'll find they're probably drill sticks.

MANN: But nothing to do with this afternoon?

SUPERINTENDENT: Good lord, no. Whatever gave you ...
Look man, our job's to minimise tension and conflict.
We'll stick to our side of the bargain, as long as you
stick to yours. That's a promise.

MANN: *(Standing)* That'll do me. *(Stopping)* Oh. You might
be interested to know, we've arranged for two
cinemaphotographers to take a film of the proceedings.
It'll make a useful ... record, later on. *(Pause)* I
hope it keeps fine. *(He leaves.)*

SUPERINTENDENT: So do I, Mr Mann. So do I.
*(The SUPERINTENDENT sits down, strokes his moustaches
reflectively, humming a rather tuneless melody. After*

a moment, a slight knock and the HEAD CONSTABLE walks
in. The SUPERINTENDENT stands up sharply.)

HEAD CONSTABLE: All right, George. (The SUPERINTENDENT
sits down again. The HEAD CONSTABLE stands in the
doorway.) Everything ... ready for this afternoon?

SUPERINTENDENT: (Slowly) Everything, sir.

HEAD CONSTABLE: (Nodding, lips pursed) Good. (Pause) Good.

33. ACTUALITY, STILL WORK AND STUDIO COMBINED PERHAPS

MANN addressing this vast gathering from No 1 platform.
Enormous build-up of sound, songs, bands, etc., subsiding
during the speech. We cut, from time to time, to squads
of police moving at the double through deserted streets,
staves at the port.

MANN: (Throwing off coat and waistcoat) Comrades.
Citizens. It is good to see you. You lift an old
man's heart. Your spirit, your will, your courage
and the rightness of your cause will see us through.
(Great cheering.) We're gathered here today,
peacefully, to demonstrate our great determination to
win this long and terrible battle against the
employing classes and the state, their lackey. You
should know that the railwaymen have joined us, have
asked us to fight their fight for them. Now, all the
transport workers of Liverpool are arm-in-arm against
the class enemy. We have sent a letter to
the employers, asking for an early settlement of our
grievances, and a speedy return to work. If that
brings forth no satisfactory reply, if they ignore us,
the Strike Committee advise a General Strike all
round. (Great cheering.) We cannot, in face of the
military and police drafted into the city - to say
nothing of the two gunboats sent down by the

government to clutter up the mouth of the Mersey - we
cannot, I say, have effectual picketing; and we cannot
but accept this display of force as a challenge.

34. FILM (OR CLEVER STUDIO?)

*Edges of vast crowd, near Great Nelson Street. Three or
four lads stand on shop windowsills to try and get a sight
of the platform. Two policemen appear, order them down.
The lads are loth to move. The policemen drag them
roughly down. One lad crashes badly on to a shoulder.
A section of the crowd advances on the two policemen,
edges them out of the street. Suddenly, round the
corner, a tight phalanx of forty policemen, with staves at
the port. They double silently towards the strikers, who
simply stand and watch them, incredulous. The police make
contact, crack skulls like mangoes, ruthless, disciplined,
mechanical. They show no anger; behave as soldiers doing
drill. Charge after charge occurs, a new wave building
as the first one breaks. It is terrifying. The square
is filled with shrieks and groans; the ground seethes
with wounded men, women and children. Here and there some
strikers try to organise an effective counter, but they are
outclassed and outmanoeuvred.*

35. MARITIME HALL. THAT NIGHT

*Corridors and stairway bulging with wounded. MANN picks
his way through them, giving tightlipped comfort where he
can. From lead-off rooms, the sounds of others
receiving attention. QUILLIAM steps in from the street.*
MANN: *(Sharp)* Did you see them?
QUILLIAM: Yes.
MANN: So?
QUILLIAM: Police got there first. Confiscated all the

film.

(MANN stands up, stretches, looks at nothing in particular, very tense.)

MANN: *(Finally)* They will pay. They must be made to. *(Pause)* Have you got a count?

QUILLIAM: *(From notebook)* A rough one. Thirty-five in the Northern, one hundred and forty-two at the Royal, twenty at the Southern, eleven at the Stanley, around three hundred at the East Dispensary. With what we've got on our own premises, it's about a thousand.

MANN: Police?

QUILLIAM: About a dozen. It's hard to say.

MANN: *(Bitter, tough)* We must take it ... as a lesson from history, Billie. *(Pause)* No deals ... with the state.

(He turns, picks his way upstairs, bending to comfort the injured who litter his path.)

36. FILM? TOWN HALL

Vast committee room, gleaming, oaken, emblazoned and escutcheoned. Towards the bottom of the huge table in the centre of the room sit MANN, QUILLIAM and PEARCE. Silence. They sit very still, indifferent to the room, incurious, unmoved. The top door opens and a liveried ATTENDANT, staff in hand, enters.

ATTENDANT: *(Boomy)* His Worship the Mayor.

(The MAYOR appears, in morning suit and chain. He is small, dapper, a baronet. The ATTENDANT walks him to his ornate chair at the head of the table, bangs the floor three times with the staff, pulls the chair out and backs it for the MAYOR, then retires to the door. MANN, QUILLIAM and PEARCE remain seated and inattentive throughout.)

MAYOR: Gentlemen. I'm ... very gratified you consented
to this meeting. Would you be good enough to inform
me who it is I have the pleasure of addressing?

MANN: My name is Mann. This is Mr Quilliam. This is
Mr Pearce.

MAYOR: How do you do. *(Pause)* Gentlemen, let me come to
the issue with all the expedition I can muster. When
the ... national railway strike ended in agreement
and, in consequence, the dock owners agreed to end
their lock-out of dockers, it was assumed by all men
of goodwill here in Liverpool that the transport
strike would, in fact, be at an end, and ... that ...
work would be resumed forthwith. It ... er ...
seems, at any rate to me, that employers have been ...
more than generous in acceding to your demands, not
only in respect of seafaring men, but also dockers,
carters, and all other classes of transport workers in
the port. *(Pause)* Now, I know there are one or two
grievances outstanding, but in the interests of the
community - and that includes workers' wives and
children, you won't need reminding - is it not now
possible to sanction a full return to work, pending a
satisfactory settlement of the outstanding issues?
(Pause) Gentlemen?

MANN: *(Slowly)* I speak for the Strike Committee. *(Pause)*
The answer's no.

MAYOR: Mr Mann, please see reason. There really is no
point in ...

MANN: I think you must allow us to decide whether there
is point. *(Pause)* A settlement is, as you well know,
entirely in your hands. Reinstate the three thousand
tramwaymen who struck in support of our just claims,
and we will effect a full resumption within

forty-eight hours. Unless and until that happens,
not a ship, not a cart, not a bottle of milk or
bucket of coal will move, without we say so.

MAYOR: I quite appreciate your ... loyalty to the
tramwaymen, but you must see how it stands with us.
Eight hundred men refused to strike. It would be a
gratuitous insult to their loyalty if we agreed to
reinstate unconditionally.

QUILLIAM: Equally, you should appreciate how far we have
ourselves come in this matter. We have had to resist
repeated demands from the men themselves that no
settlement should be accepted until the eight hundred
'blacklegs' were dismissed.

MAYOR: That is, of course, unthinkable.

MANN: Of course. We are agreed. *(Pause)* Is it Petrie?

MAYOR: Sir Charles *is* taking it all ... very personally.

MANN: He must learn to be more ... pragmatic. There is
no room for pride in politics. Perhaps you need a
new chairman for your Highways Committee.

MAYOR: Sir Charles is a very powerful man.

MANN: I'd be surprised if he remained one. *(Pause)* I hear
the Board of Trade have called him down to London. Is
that so?

MAYOR: Well ... Sir Charles *is* in London at the moment.
Whether it is to talk over matters at the ...

MANN: *(Standing)* Good. That will do *us*, I think,
Mr Mayor. Mr Askwith will tweak his nose for him.
The tramwaymen will be back by the weekend. If you're
a wagering man, place your sovereigns on it.

MAYOR: *(Standing)*   I shouldn't be too sure of that,
Mr Mann.

MANN: *(Smiling faintly)* Sometimes I wonder how you get
where you do, you people. You read the world like a

124

page of Swahili in the dark. Sir Charles is not a
very powerful man. He is a jackal among puppies. Now
he has fallen among tigers, you will hear nothing but
the tearing of flesh. The strike is all but over.
Take my word for it. Good day, Mr Mayor.
*(MANN walks out, fast and straight, PEARCE and
QUILLIAM flanking him. The ATTENDANT opens the door
sharply. The MAYOR looks dismally round at their
backs.)*

37. EXT. FILM. LIME STREET STATION. EARLY MORNING
MANN and QUILLIAM on the platform, a train in.
QUILLIAM: Straight back, is it?
MANN: Aye. I'm due in Paris Monday. Conference.
QUILLIAM: It's been good.
MANN: Yes. Not a bad 72 days. We'll do better, though.
QUILLIAM: Keep in touch.
MANN: Mmm. *(Hand out.)* Goodbye, brother.
QUILLIAM: *(Taking it)* Goodbye. Tom.
    *(MANN walks down platform, grip in hand. The
    SUPERINTENDENT and a CONSTABLE step out from the
    shadow.)*
SUPERINTENDENT: *(Easily)* Morning, Mr Mann.
MANN: *(Halting; hard)* You got business with me?
SUPERINTENDENT: Yes we have, Mr Mann.
MANN: Well?
SUPERINTENDENT: It's going to take a bit of time. You'll
    have to forget this one *(At train)*, I'm afraid.
MANN: Oh? Have you got a charge?
SUPERINTENDENT: Oh yes indeed. Had it drawn up myself.
    Incitement to mutiny.
MANN: What?
SUPERINTENDENT: The article you published in your paper.

You know: Don't shoot on your fellow workers. We're
having you. *(Nice smile.)* I'm pleased to say. *(Pause)*
Shall we go?
(They walk off, MANN between TWO POLICEMEN. Fade.
Fade up:)

38. CELL BELOW COURT

MANN sits in it alone. After a while, QUILLIAM, in court
dress, arrives outside the door, is let in.

QUILLIAM: Well. There we are.

MANN: *(Quiet, impassive)* Aye.

QUILLIAM: I'm sorry. I handled it badly. I didn't
    expect ...

MANN: No, Billie. You did fine. Really. I could do
    with nine months' rest. *(A small grin.)*

QUILLIAM: Erm ... Ellen's here.

MANN: Aye. Does she ...? *(Nodding)* Show her in, then,
    will you, Billie?
    (QUILLIAM knocks on cell door, is released, the door
    closes. MANN stands and faces the door. It stays
    shut a long time. It opens finally and ELLEN MANN
    enters. She's late forties, small, grey, tired,
    dowsed. She speaks with a Suffolk accent still, after
    all these years. She is hesitant, tiredly in control,
    but a little bewildered.)

MANN: Hello, Ellen.

ELLEN: Hello, Tom.

MANN: How've you been, love?

ELLEN: All right. Are you ...?

MANN: Yes, I'm fine.
    (Long silence.)

ELLEN: Mr Quilliam said you might appeal or something.

MANN: Aye. We might. Don't fret.

126